The Caveman in the Mirror

Michael T. Mulligan

ISBN: 1508844801
ISBN-13: 9781508844808

DEDICATION

And the credit goes to...

Top credit for this book goes to my mother, Gloria Delores Mulligan. I would like to recognize her own faith journey, her daily commitment to prayer and church attendance, and her constant encouragement. There were those few times growing up when she chased me and my unruly brothers around the house with a shoe in her hand, yelling, "I don't mean maybe!" It was hard to take her too seriously. In my adult life, I look to her for guidance. I trust her 100% and I trust the One she follows 100%. She's one special lady.

I would like to recognize my loving wife, Helen Marie, who holds my hand and keeps my heart warm, especially on cold winter nights in our new home state of Iowa. She supports my calling to write daily and graciously gives me the moral support I need to accomplish all God asks of me.

To my children, Ryan, Nicole and Shane, I thank you for all the sacrifices you endure putting up with my writing deadlines. Each of you inherited the writing gene prevalent in our family for countless generations. I encourage you to nurture the talent you have within you and to write compelling stories with life lessons for future readers in the generations yet to come.

To my extended family, my ancestors and to the lost members of our family tree who have been recently found, thanks for sharing your lives with me. Thank you, cousin John, for endorsing this book and for encouraging me to keep stretching out of my comfort zone.

A big shout out goes to cousin Mark, founder of Castaway Kids, and author of **The Three Miracles**. Thanks for bringing your music to my new home state and for being my first visitor after my relocation. I will keep encouraging my readers to send a couple of pesos your way in support of your charitable works south of the border.

To the Angels in the Outfield who believed in me when I wrote my first book, I say thank you. You will always be in my heart.

Special thanks to the team at Elite Sports in Parnell, Iowa for your outstanding efforts bringing the caveman to life on the front cover. You came through big time when the pressure was on.

And to those who are reading this book, I say thank you. All of us in this world are filled with questions. We each have our own journey and our own purpose. Thanks for sharing the road with me and for taking the time to read this book.

Chapter One

The people walking in darkness have seen a great light; on those living in the land of the shadow of death a light has dawned. ~ Isaiah 9:2

"We're all going to die!" Peter's words were barely audible over the crashing waves battering their tiny fishing boat in an uneven rhythm like a song peppered with sharp notes in all the wrong places. The twelve were living a nightmare while their Master slept on a cushion in the stern, his rapid-eye movement appearing to harmonize with each blast of wind.

The full moon disappeared intermittently behind the fast-moving clouds making it almost impossible to see. When a brief opening appeared in the sky, the whitecaps in the middle of the Sea of Galilee became visible monsters with bright shaggy highlights on top of their heads, each one hammering the under-sized fishing boat. It didn't matter that four of the followers were experienced commercial fisherman; they were outmatched by the squalls suddenly appearing out of nowhere on a relatively calm night, turning the area into some type of Devil's Triangle.

Andrew, the oldest member of the group, was overcome with seasickness and leaned over the side of the boat, spewing his dinner into the water. Peter, yelled out to him, "hang on, brother!" James and John cupped their hands together to bail water while the others clung to the boat using death grips.

Nathaniel inched over to Jesus, crawling on all fours, while the boat rocked like a cradle. The last obstacle was Thomas. His tucked fetal position made him look like a giant ball bouncing around inside a pinball machine. Thomas was trying to block out the sound of the screeching winds with his head buried between both ears. The waves pelted incessantly. Nathaniel worked his way around Thomas and wedged himself between the two men. The boat looked like it could capsize at any moment.

"Wake up, Jesus," Nathaniel hollered while shaking him. "We need you." A wave swept over the bow and engulfed Jesus like a jug of Gatorade dumped on a victorious coach at the end of a football game. At last, Jesus opened his eyes and smiled at Nathaniel, seemingly unaware of all the danger his followers were in. The moon peered through a hole in the clouds, shining a spotlight on the boat from directly above. When the followers saw that Jesus was awake, they yelled out, "teacher, don't you care if we drown?"

Jesus got up, rebuked the wind, and said to the waves, "Quiet! Be still!" The wind died down and everything became calm. Thomas uncurled and sat up for the first time since the storm struck. Several minutes passed before anyone spoke. Jesus looked off towards the north shoreline. A lone jackal was howling far off but only Jesus could hear him. He turned toward Peter and directed him to change course before returning to his cushion and going back to sleep for the rest of the night.

Peter kept watch while the others huddled in pairs to stay warm. Their soaking wet clothes had a stench of rotting fish from weeks on the road with Jesus. Nathaniel cracked a few jokes to keep the mood light. Matthew spent most of his life on dry land collecting taxes before he met Jesus. He appeared to be the most relieved when Jesus calmed the storm, yet too embarrassed to tell the others he didn't know how to swim. He wasn't the only member of the twelve with a deficiency.

Chapter Two

The creature stood up on his hind legs, poised on a look-out point fifty yards above the north shores of the Sea of Galilee. He bellowed half-animal and half-human screams that echoed throughout the ravine. When the followers first heard the shrills, they wanted to turn their fishing boat around and head home. Jesus was unrelenting. He urged the group to paddle in the direction of the cackles while he remained standing at the stern with his arms crossed.

***

The early morning sun lit up the horizon, revealing extensive damage to the fishing vessel. The mast was broken apart. Remnants of the tattered sail flapped in the light wind like a white surrender flag. The dreary eyes of all the passengers fixated in the direction of the screeches but they were still too far away to identify the source of the commotion. No one spoke, not even Peter, the man who loved the sound of his own words. Never before had the group been so close to death. They were tired and weak. The last thing they wanted was another life-threatening event. The hairs raising on their arms each time the voice in the wilderness cried out foretold of another danger lurking in the distance.

The creature peered at the group as they landed on the shoreline, showing his canines like a rabid dog. Jesus took the lead and asked his followers to hike behind him. The trail up the gorge was filled with loose rock making the ascent challenging, especially in wet leather sandals. John, the most athletic of the group, stayed the closest to Jesus until he lost his footing near the top and tumbled backwards. Philip broke his fall and propped John back up in time to see Jesus confront the monster, coiled up like a king cobra about to attack. Jesus raised his hands and commanded the creature to rise. The response was immediate. The naked man stood in a hunched over position, brandishing broken chains on both wrists and ankles. The putrid smell coming from his body was like rotten eggs. There were scratches and bruises from head to toe. The beast's black scraggly hair reached all the way to his tail bone. His light blue eyes were a gateway to his tormented soul. They stared at Jesus as he came closer.

* * *

The disciples formed a semi-circle behind Jesus about twenty yards away from the spectacle, their eyes locked onto the crazed outcast. Both men were in a stare-down contest. The cave dweller was the first to break the silence. "Son of the Most High God, why do you torment me?" He growled.

"Who are you?" Jesus asked.

"Legions!" the demoniac spewed from his parched lips in a raspy voice, meaning multiple devils. He hissed at Jesus while looking down at his feet. Some villagers who were tending to a herd of 1,000 pigs nearby witnessed the scuffle from their grazing area and drew closer to get a better view. They knew the caveman was dangerous and kept their distance.

The unclothed man lurched forward. Jesus held up his right hand and ordered him to halt. The creature froze with fear. The crowd was stunned at Jesus' spell-bounding power over the attacker. Without speaking, Jesus aimed his right index finger at the creature's face and lowered his hand to the ground. The beast lowered his head and kneeled before Jesus in quiet surrender. His nose touched the ground and his grubby fingers clawed at the clay dirt while he panted in an uneven rhythm.

"Depart!" Jesus commanded, pointing to the lake. The demoniac sat up and shook his head from side to side.

"Please," the demons shouted with one voice. “We beg you, Son of the Most High God, do not send us back. We would rather be with the pigs."

Jesus pointed to the pigs. The caveman rose up and danced like a puppet on strings before collapsing like a rag doll. A small dust devil swirled around the lifeless man before heading directly towards the swine. Immediately, the pigs began screaming as if they were on fire. They were running around in circles, slamming into each other like drunk rugby players. The villagers became afraid and ran for cover while the baffled pigs stampeded towards the lake. Fifty at a time, the herd plunged over the cliff, squealing and grunting uncontrollably before drowning in the lake below.

The villagers fled the scene in fear. The twelve apostles hiked over to the edge of the cliff where the pigs disappeared leaving Jesus alone with the man who was unconscious. Jesus retreated to the fishing boat and pulled out a white robe and a second pair of sandals he reserved for special occasions like weddings. He retrieved a fishing knife, a wash cloth and a pottery vase he filled with water from the lake. James and John came over to the boat to check on Jesus.

"Men, we need to get this boat repaired," Jesus said, pointing to the broken mast and the tattered sail. "Can you please gather the group and work together to restore it?"

***

The men had many questions about what they observed but were too afraid to talk about it. James responded, "yes master, we will make the repairs."

Jesus climbed back up to the spot where he left the unkempt stranger, still sleeping. He waved his hands over the chains and they unsnapped. Then, he dipped the wash cloth in the vase and wiped the grunge off the man's body. With each swiping motion, the scars and scratches faded until they were completely gone. Jesus used his fingers to comb the man's hair, carefully untangling all the knots. He pulled out his fishing knife and used it to trim the man's hair, mustache and beard.

When the man woke up, Jesus smiled and said to him, "behold, I make all things new." The man pulled the white robe over his shoulders and sat down on a large boulder located just outside the cave he had been living in for the last year. Jesus bent down and placed the sandals on his feet.

"You *are* the Messiah, aren't you?"

"Yes, Bedrock."

The man look puzzled. "Bedrock?"

"From now on you will be called Bedrock. You are the secret rock hidden from my people who will be a part of my Father's plan. You are to remain here, separated from the chosen ones. You will publish all the good that I have done for you."

Bedrock buried his head in his hands and began weeping uncontrollably. Jesus put his arm on his shoulder and said, "Do not be sad. Your wife and son are sleeping. Chara and Caleb will be waking up soon and you will see them again."

"What are you saying, Jesus? How can this be true? My pregnant wife was murdered when the invaders destroyed my village."

Jesus repeated himself. "Chara and Caleb are sleeping. You will see them again."

"I have a son?"

"Yes. He has your wife's blue-green eyes and your black wavy hair. The invaders did not take her with the other female captives because she was pregnant. I know when you returned home after searching for work, you saw something horrific. Your village was burned to the ground and everyone you loved was either dead or taken away as slaves. You lost all hope. The moment you began to hate is the moment the demons took possession of your body and mind. These demons were once beautiful angels in my Father's kingdom. They made a choice to end their relationship with my Father and they were cast out. They scour the planet looking for people like you who are without love in their hearts. Your hatred was their portal. My Father sent me to come here and heal you. He has big plans for you. I have known you since you were under the fig tree."

Bedrock already knew more about Jesus in thirty minutes than the others who had been with Jesus for nearly three years. The demons gave Bedrock a special insight about Jesus. They tricked Bedrock into believing it was Jesus who could have saved everyone in the village if he had come sooner but chose to let the barbarians have their way.

"Why did you allow Chara and Caleb to be murdered, Jesus?"

"My Father created His children in perfect love. That means you must have the free will to choose your own path. The demons who are in this world already made their choice. Their days are numbered. They want to take as many souls with them as possible. There are dark days ahead. In the end, I will make all things new just as I have made you new today."

The village people heard about the pigs and banded together with sticks and stones to confront Jesus and the caveman. The apostles saw the lynch mob approaching and rushed back to stand behind their leader in a show of force.

The village leader looked down at the lake and saw the pigs floating in the water. Some of them were already washing up on the shoreline. The followers were careful to keep their distance from the dead pigs as they were considered unclean. These villagers were unfamiliar with Jewish laws regarding pigs. The loss of 1,000 pigs meant trouble for their economy.

"You and your men must leave," the leader said. "You are not welcome here."

Jesus paused for a moment with his head down. Then, he turned around slowly and asked his followers to depart.

"Take me with you, master," the caveman said. The village people did not recognize him in his white garment and his freshly cut hair. They were surprised the man could speak at all because he never uttered a coherent word in front of them until that moment.

Jesus pulled the man away from the crowd and whispered in his ear, "Bedrock, you cannot follow me. If you stay with me you will get in the way of my Father's plan for me and your testimony about who I am will stop the Crucifixion. Without a Crucifixion, there can be no Resurrection; without a Resurrection, your wife and son cannot ever wake up. These men who are with me, most of them are fishermen. They don't really know me. I need it to stay this way until I am reunited with my Father. I promise I will return to this area one more time before my final hour. Your place is here with these people. Stay with them and remember you are to publish all the good I have done for you. Okay?"

Peter and Judas were hoping for a fight with the angry villagers. Instead, they watched their master hug the caveman good-bye and turn away from the nervous crowd. Jesus and the twelve proceeded back down the canyon, climbed into the boat and cast off, heading to the furthest point north on the Sea of Galilee. They made sure to stay clear of the dead pigs bobbing in the water all around them. Eventually, the crowd retreated to their village, leaving the caveman all alone.

Bedrock wandered off to a rocky area where rainwater had accumulated in a small pool. He leaned down to sip water from the pool and noticed his reflection. His clean-cut appearance reminded him of Chara and the special times they had together. He remembered how he fell in love with her when she was a slave girl working for a benevolent family. They gave her many liberties and she used her free time to be with her man. Bedrock scrounged enough money from odd jobs to purchase Chara and set her free. They were both Greek Hellenists who believed there were gods, however, slave girls like Chara understood the gods paid little attention to slaves. Bedrock was always too busy earning a living to study Greek culture. Today's encounter with the Messiah opened his eyes and he was filled with new hope.

While Bedrock was studying his reflection in the water, the cloud covering the sun moved away. The sunlight bounced off the water right into Bedrock's blue eyes, leaving him blinded for a few moments. Bedrock squeezed his eyes shut and then opened them again. After a few minutes, his vision returned. He looked back into the pool and saw a strange vision.

Chapter Three

Six weeks passed before the man dared to confront his haggard reflection one more time. The man's hands became clammy and drops of sweat rolled down his face. He closed his eyes and prayed nothing bad would happen. Even though his eyes were closed, he could still see the original reflection that haunted his dreams at night and followed him everywhere he went during the day. He was still too afraid to tell anyone about the caveman in the mirror. Not even his own wife.

Slowly, he opened his eyes. There he was; his reflection was in the same spot, waiting for him to reappear like a puppy dog waiting for his master to come home from work. The sunlight made it difficult to see more than a silhouette. The clouds rolled in and covered up the sun making it easier to get a better view. The man drew closer to his reflection. He noticed his alter-ego dressed in a white robe. The four shackles with broken chains on the ankles and wrists were gone. While staring at the image, the man rubbed his right hand over his chin and felt the whiskers from his straggly face. The man on the other side appeared to be clean-shaven and his hair was neat in appearance.

The gentle blue eyes staring back at him were different. No longer did they appear crazed like the first time he saw them six weeks ago. The man wondered if this image was the same person. It was hard to tell. Even the scratches that crisscrossed the man's face and once naked body were now invisible.

There were no buildings on the other side. The landscape appeared undeveloped. It was prime real estate overlooking a lake. Other than the reflection, there were no people. The man on the other side was as still as a rabbit. The expression on his face was like a game show contestant struggling to get the right answer.

***

"What are you doing?" Marie asked her husband, entering the room with a handful of empty boxes.

The image in the mirror vanished before Marie could see anything. "Just thinking about my ancestors," Thomas replied, startled she appeared so abruptly.

Thomas always shared everything with his wife and he was uncomfortable keeping secrets from Marie. He didn't know if he was going crazy or if perhaps he stumbled upon a strange new world. He felt uneasy about staring into the mirror. Everything on the other side seemed so real. *Who was this stranger in the mirror and why was he haunting me?* Thomas thought as he composed himself. He wasn't ready to tell his wife about the caveman.

"I need help," Marie said, pointing to a column of storage boxes she loaded with clothes from their bedroom closet. "The realtor will be showing our house tomorrow and we need to move everything to the garage. What's wrong with your face? You look like you might be getting sick."

Thomas wiped the sweat off his face with a towel and reached down to pick up a couple of boxes. "I'm okay, honey. Just exhausted from all the packing."

"You better get to bed early tonight, Thomas. I need you healthy so we can get the packing done. Maybe you can knock it off for a while with your genealogy project. Geez. Nobody's going anywhere...they're all dead. And you're going to be dead too if you don't get this place picked up before we show the house."

Thomas didn't answer. The ancestry project was not a good topic of conversation. It was time consuming and he knew he didn't have extra time to be researching his family roots in the middle of a move. As he walked down the stairs of their California home, he stopped and looked at the giant mirror hanging above the fireplace. He was relieved that no one was on the other side staring back at him, however, he was frightened by all that was happening.

Marie and their youngest son, Michael, often complained about hearing footsteps in the middle of the night. The Morgans did not learn their home was built on top of an ancient Indian burial site until after they purchased their dream home. Marie suspected the thumps she and Michael were hearing might be related to graves below her dream home. Thomas knew if he talked to his family about his visions it would only add strength to their belief that their home was haunted. Besides, once the house sold it wouldn't matter if the house was haunted. They would leave all their skeletons in the closet and live happily ever after without any ghosts.

Thomas was sorting through his collection of books to be packed and came across a gift his youngest sister gave him for Christmas. His mind drifted back to the last time he talked with Sacha about her desire to explore other faiths. Some friends of hers were tempting her to join their group. They argued the church she belonged to had a breakdown early in its history and never fully recovered, prompting the need for a new religion to restore order. Thomas didn't know enough about the early church to guide his sister so he said a little prayer to find the right things to say to her. The answer came in a dream a few nights later. The place was Antioch. When Thomas woke up, he asked his wife, "do you know what's going on in Antioch?"

"No, Thomas. Is it in California?" she asked.

Thomas couldn't recall where Antioch was located but he was sure something was going on there. Judging by the scenery in his dream, he thought maybe it was somewhere in the California desert. The terrain was rugged and the vegetation sparse. There was a dried up riverbed that served as a sandy beach area for the group that appeared to be camped out in the middle of nowhere. There was a guy in a red robe who was doing a lot of talking but he wasn't the leader. The rest of the group wore white robes and appeared to be broken up into to groups of two. The dream was so vivid that it didn't feel like a dream. It was more like a vision. "Maybe you should turn on the news," Marie suggested.

Thomas kissed Marie good-bye and headed off to his job at a publishing company, eager to get to the bottom of his strange premonition. The whole day he asked his customers if they heard any news about Antioch. At the end of the day, one of his teammates at his publishing job overheard Thomas talking about his dream and said to him, "Thomas, there's an Antioch in the Bible. It's the first place where the followers of Jesus were called

Christians."

Thomas picked up the phone and called his wife. "Honey, Antioch is in the Bible. Can you please find our Bible and read up on it? It's the place where the followers of Jesus were first called Christians." He spoke so fast Marie could barely understand him.

"Hello to you, too, Thomas," Marie said sarcastically. Thomas was so focused on Antioch that he skipped over the usual questions about his wife's day.

"Sorry, honey. I'm in a big rush to make deadline and I wanted to share what I learned from Ross. He seems to know a lot about the Bible. Do you mind doing a quick look-up while I'm holding?"

Thomas stayed on the line while Marie searched for their Bible. It was in pristine condition and only used when the Morgans travelled to a christian camp in the San Bernadino mountains for their annual summer vacations. Marie got back on the line after she located the Bible and asked, "Thomas, where do I need to look to find Antioch?"

Thomas turned to Ross and asked, "What section is Antioch in?"

Ross studied the Bible daily and he knew it inside out. He directed Thomas and his wife to the New Testament. Marie fumbled through the pages but couldn't find any references to Antioch. Thomas grew impatient. He had a deadline to meet and needed to hang up. "Marie, keep looking. I'll be home soon and we'll talk more about this."

Thomas rushed home as soon as his work was done. When he walked in from the garage, Marie already had the Bible open to the passage about Antioch. She was eager to find out why this was so important to her husband.

Thomas kissed his wife and then sat down with her to go over the passage. His eyes grew wide as he studied the chapter. Everything matched up to the dream including a reference to a man named John Mark. Could it be that God was giving Thomas answers to his prayers by sending him dreams? Suddenly, Thomas felt he needed to dig deeper. He needed to learn everything he could about Antioch. He resolved to learn as much as possible about the history of the church. He dedicated one hour every morning to studying the Bible. He was so methodical about his daily Bible reading routine that his wife poked fun at him, at times calling him Thomas the robot. For two years, Thomas scoured the Bible every morning at sunrise. Marie knew that when he was engrossed in his reading, Thomas was in a trance, almost like a zombie. She gave up trying to talk to him because his mind was too far away.

The sound of the cork popping on the Cabernet Sauvignon snapped Thomas out of his daydream about Antioch. Thomas did his best to be in the moment. Deep down he knew there was a relationship between the Antioch dream from two years ago and the visions of the caveman in his bathroom mirror. Thomas looked into Marie's eyes and grinned, pretending to be in the moment with her.

"Here's to our new buyers," Marie said, "let's hope they fall in love with our place tomorrow make an offer the banks can't refuse."

"The fourth time is a charm," Thomas said, half-smiling as he raised his glass. The process of selling a home in a down market was overwhelming and the banks already turned down three other buyers in the last twelve months. "I have a feeling we're headed in a new direction and when this short sale is finally approved we can close out another chapter of our lives. One way or another, our days in California are numbered," Marie said.

Chapter Four

Thomas opened his eyes in the darkness and peeked over Marie's shoulders to check on the time. It was 3:00 AM. He thought about the early morning appointment the couple had with the new buyers while he laid on his back for several minutes. Marie was sleeping quietly. A lone bird was chirping a pleasant serenade outside.

Thomas reached for his Bible on the nightstand and climbed out of bed. He stubbed his toe on one of the moving boxes on his way to the corner of the bedroom where his favorite chair was located, almost waking up Marie. He cupped his right hand over his mouth to muffle the sound of his groans and made his way to the chair in the darkness. The swivel chair was round and rotated in a circular motion. The cushions were extra soft, making it an ideal place for an afternoon nap. The couple often fought for time on the chair and the first one up in the morning won. Thomas sat down on the chair, turned on his LED book light and opened up his Bible. He tried to take his mind off the pain he was feeling from his big toe by saying a prayer.

Thomas used his prayer time to guide him before turning to a random passage of the Bible. The lack of order in his reading made his study time interesting. He trusted the Holy Spirit would lead him to the best material for the day. Thomas prayed, *Holy Spirit, please show me who I am in God's eyes.* He stopped flipping through the pages at chapter eight from St. Luke in his Latin Vulgate Bible. This version was a spur-of-the-moment online purchase he made without knowing how difficult it was to follow. His Vulgate Bible was filled with all kinds of "Thees" and "Thous." The words were translated directly from the Hebrew Bible to Latin in the late 4th century. Thomas had no clue there were so many different versions but he was too frugal to spend his money on a more modern translation.

Thomas couldn't believe what he was reading. There

he was. The caveman, wearing nothing but chains on his ankles and wrists. He was the splitting image of the naked caveman who barged into Thomas' life six months earlier. Thomas was frozen. His jaw dropped. According to the Bible passage, the caveman was a demoniac, meaning he was possessed by multiple demons. There was no doubt in Thomas' mind that the caveman in the Bible was the same person showing up in his bathroom mirror. Thomas had an uncanny ability to recognize people, even when they wore disguises. Marie often remarked he would be a good fit for the C.I.A.

Thomas read on. His hands were so shaky he could barely read the words. He wondered if the devils haunting the caveman in the story were responsible for re-incarnating themselves inside their home. "We've got to sell this home," Thomas grumbled.

"Thomas, are you okay?" Marie asked when she heard Thomas muttering.

Thomas didn't answer. He was back in a trance. He kept reading. According to the passage, Jesus met the demoniac, cast out the demons, and healed him. The evil spirits were cast into some pigs and drowned when they jumped off a cliff. Jesus put a white garment on the caveman and removed his chains. Then Jesus left the man to "publish" all the good Jesus had done for him.

Thomas dropped the Bible. It was the light bulb moment. He knew something supernatural was going on. Thomas and the caveman were both *publishers*. And the two were somehow bound to each other.

"Ground control to Major Tom, can you hear me?" Marie asked, snapping her fingers in front of Thomas. "Take your protein pills and put your helmet on, we need to get ready for the buyers. And don't forget to take a shower. You've got some big circles under your eyes. You're looking awfully scraggly."

Chapter Five

Thomas walked past the bathroom mirror keeping his eyes focused on the tumbled travertine floor tiles. He turned on the shower and stared out the window while pondering what he read. The early morning sun was lighting up the horizon. He left the vent off so the mist would fog up the mirror and keep the caveman away. A vapor cloud filled up the bathroom and Thomas stepped into the steamy shower. "I know who you are," Thomas whispered to himself, referring to the demoniac in Luke's story. "And I'm going to find out why you're messing with me."

Marie noticed the steam building up in the bathroom and walked in to turn the vent on. Thomas had his eyes closed and didn't notice Marie standing outside the glass shower door. "Hurry up, Thomas. We have a lot to do before the buyers show up and I need a shower too."

Thomas didn't respond. The water muffled Marie's voice and Thomas couldn't hear her. Marie opened the door and tapped on Thomas' shoulder. Thomas rinsed the shampoo out of his eyes and turned to his wife who was growing impatient. "You forgot to turn on the vent again, Thomas. And we're running out of time. The buyers will be here in no time. Can you pick up the pace a little?"

Thomas shut off the water and toweled off. He skipped brushing his teeth or putting on deodorant, afraid if he looked into the mirror again his ghost would return. "Please Lord, let these people be the right buyers for our home," Thomas prayed as he got dressed.

The doorbell rang. Thomas took a deep breath before opening it. The family usually stayed away during showings but time was running out and they needed the weekends to finish packing. The moving truck was scheduled and there was no turning back. These buyers were the last hope of avoiding foreclosure and Thomas knew the pressure was on.

Thomas opened the door. Two men and a young girl smiled at Thomas and extended their hands for a greeting. "I'm Scott and this is my daughter, Mandy. This is my realtor, Bruce. Is it okay if we look at your home? Bruce had a stack of papers and pulled out a pen before asking a series of questions.

"Is this your whole family? Thomas asked.

"My wife, Patty and my other two children are still in Montana," Scott answered. "We've been trying to buy a home in the area for six months and the process has been rough. My wife knows what we both want and she is tired of flying back and forth. She told me find us a home soon or forget about California."

"Please come in and look around," Thomas said. "My wife is around here somewhere packing. We'll stay out of your way while you check the place out."

Bruce opened up his notebook and asked about the listing. "I'm glad you're here, Thomas. I just wanted to verify this is a short sale. Scott and Patty are a little timid about making an offer on a short sale because the banks keep getting in the way."

"Yes, Bruce, this is a short sale. I'll be up front with you. This house has been our family home for over twenty years. I'm in the publishing business and the industry is in a tailspin. I can't afford to be here any longer. Eighteen months ago I called my bank to tell them I need out. Three other families wanted this place. The banks dragged their feet so long that all three families walked away. I got so pissed off that I stopped paying my mortgage. I told them I'm sick and tired of their games. I told them they could have the keys -- Marie and I are planning on moving out of state. They asked me to be patient. If Scott and Patty like the place, I'll do everything in my power to help you. I just want you to know another family is going to be here in about an hour. We are getting lots of traffic since the price reduction."

"$375,000, right?" the agent asked.

"Yes. That's about $300,000 below our highest appraisal." Thomas answered.

"Look, dad, there's no white anywhere on the walls," Mandy said. "And my room has the same red color I wanted in my room."

"That's Teresa's room," Thomas said. "Our daughter picked out the color herself. She's away at school right now."

Scott seemed happy with the colors and told Thomas he was sick of all the white walls he was seeing at all the other properties.

When they entered the bathroom, Thomas was careful

to avoid looking at the mirror. "Look at these tiles," Thomas said, pointing the the tumbled travertine so he could keep his attention off the mirror. "This is a versailles pattern."

"It blends really nice with the granite counter tops," Scott said.

"It's too bad this is a short sale," Bruce volunteered, closing his notebook. "We have to get moving. We have a full day of homes to preview today and my buyers are wary about short sales. I suggested they check your place out because the price reduction seems tantalizing.

The threesome hurried out the door and departed.

Marie came in from the back patio and looked at Thomas.

"How did it go, honey? They didn't stay very long."

"Doubtful, my love. They showed up without the wife and the realtor said they got beat out three different times in the short sale process. I got a voice mail from our realtor and we have another showing in about a half hour. Let's hope the next people are a better match."

"Don't worry, Thomas. Two weeks from today we are loading up the moving truck and we are out of here."

Chapter Six

"Honey, I've got great news. We got an offer. Amber and Nate are coming over to get our signatures in about an hour. They were on the phone with the agent that stopped by yesterday morning with the father-daughter buyers and everything looks super strong."

* * *

"What did our agents say about the offer?" Marie asked.

"They didn't have time to talk. The buyer's wife will be on a plane tomorrow once we sign the contract. Amber told them if they want the house they need to hustle, otherwise, the banks will take over and a foreclosure will be messy."

Marie sat down at the dining room table and looked into her husband's eyes. "Thomas, let's slow down for a minute and pray. Will you hold my hand?"

Marie started the prayer. "Heavenly Father, please hear us. I'm at the end of my rope today and both of us need you now more than ever. We ask you to please hold everything together. Please give us everything we need to break free from this situation and lead us out of this dark tunnel to a place where your light shines brightly upon us."

Thomas gripped Marie's hands tightly and added to his wife's prayer. "We trust you Father. We know you have a plan for us. We are both running out of gas. Please strengthen us. Please comfort us. Please allow this deal to close."

Thomas opened his eyes and smiled. "I'm feeling good about this one, my lady."

"It doesn't matter how you feel, Thomas, it's what the banks think that matters."

Marie's face looked tired. The roller coaster ride had taken its toll on her and she was at the end of her rope. She left all the phone conversations with the bank to Thomas. Every time an offer came in, another bank representative was involved. The process turned into a three ring circus. Unfortunately there were no clowns with happy faces. The couple just sat there without speaking. The doorbell broke the silence.

"Hello, Morgans," Amber said as she hugged Thomas and Marie. Nate followed his wife, carrying a stack of papers. Amber was the listing agent and her husband was the internet marketing specialist. They were one of the best husband and wife teams in the area. Despite their rigorous real estate schedules, both managed to stay fit. Amber wore high heels to make herself look taller than 5'2". Her calves were well defined from all her hours on the tennis courts. Nate was a black belt in Karate. He looked like Chief Inspector Clouseau from the Pink Panther with his patented mustache.

"We have a lot to do, Morgans," Amber said as she led the group to the dining room table in the rear part of the house. Thomas headed for the mini refrigerator under the island and opened it up while the other three sat down.

"Anyone care for a drink?" Thomas asked.

Nate was already spreading the paperwork across the table and Amber was ready to present the offer.

* * *

"No thanks," Amber replied. "Nate and I need to input a lot of information into the computer tonight and then prepare a report for your bank."

Nate frowned. He spent a great deal of time in Germany and was never one to turn down a cold beer but he knew his wife was right about the workload that was in front of them.

"Can you please pour me a glass of wine, honey?" Marie asked.

Thomas poured a glass of Chardonnay for his wife and helped himself to a can of beer before taking a seat at the head of the table.

Amber led the discussion. "These people really want your house. They are offering full price. They also want most of your furniture. I told them you can work that out in a separate agreement. They are asking for a 30 day escrow."

"What about the wife?" Thomas asked. "Doesn't she need to see the house first?"

"The husband took a bunch of pictures when he came through on Saturday and sent them to his wife. She fell in love with the pictures. Their daughter already has her bedroom picked out. Apparently, they have been beat out so many times that the wife told her husband to find a place without her. He is sharing an apartment with a friend down the hill and the place is cramped. Their only concern is our bank. I assured them I know what to do and I can handle the process. Their agent is a personal friend and he is not up to speed on short sales. Between him, Nate and me, we can get this done. Your banker started paying more attention when you two decided to stop paying on your mortgage. Your credit is shot and it will be three years before you will be able to buy another property. That beats having a foreclosure on your record, doesn't it?"

Marie leaned in to the table and asked, "what about signing all the documents at closing? We will be on the road and we don't even know where we will be staying."

Amber replied, "We have a secure website to handle everything. Nate will be in charge of sending you the documents online."

"It doesn't look like there is anything to counter here," Thomas said while sipping his Bud Light.

"These people are serious. They already have a property inspector lined up and they want to come back for measurements. The wife will be here tomorrow night. She will meet with you next weekend to discuss the furniture."

Marie raised her wine glass to Thomas and said, "Dear God, thank you. And please watch over Amber and Nate. Please guide them during this process."

***

Amber presented the contract with precision and the couple signed everything in a clock-wise direction. Nate was in charge of putting everything in place once the contract was signed. When the couple stood up to depart, Roxy, the Chihuahua adopted from Mexico, came rushing out from the back bedroom and started barking like an attack dog. At six pounds, she wasn't much of a threat. The Morgan's other dog, Lucky, observed the commotion from his bed in the corner of the family room. He rarely got up, leaving the guard duty to Roxy. Lucky was a fourteen-year-old Australian shepherd/ Border collie mix breed with short hair and long legs. Ever since he lost his companion, Lady, a sheltie who looked like a miniature Lassie, he lost his spunk. Roxy took over as the alpha dog and she chased the real estate duo right out the front door.

Thomas walked over to Lucky and bent down to check on him. Lucky seemed to know that things were about to change.

Chapter Seven

Thomas sat down for a few minutes next to the hole he was digging in the backyard. He looked at the large boulder that he and his children rolled on top of Lady's grave one year earlier. A light wind blew in his face. Thomas turned around to look at the yard where his children and his dogs played when they were growing up.

A bee buzzed by him and inspected a yellow flower sprouting on top of a weed near the boulder. Thomas recalled how Lucky loved to chase the bees, jumping up and down and biting at them as they pollinated the plants every Spring.

Marie came outside and offered Thomas a glass of cold water. She took a seat on a large rock next to Thomas and looked at the hole.

"Lucky is ready to be with Lady," Marie said. "I offered him a treat but he won't even raise his head from his bed."

Thomas nodded in agreement and sipped on the water. "This ground is really hard to dig through, Marie. It's going to take another hour. Did you make the appointment?"

"The vet said you can stop by anytime today."

Tears filled Marie's eyes. The reality of the moment tugged at her heart. Thomas wrapped his arms around Marie and comforted her.

"Marie, do you remember the day Lucky brought that gopher he caught inside the house?"

Marie wiped the tears from her eyes and laughed. "I wanted to kill him. There was blood everywhere. Then I looked at him wagging his tail and saw how happy he was. He was so proud. I'm really going to miss him."

***

"Honey, I'm just thankful the new homeowners love dogs as much as we do. It was kind of them to let us keep Lady and Lucky together. They said goodbye to their dog before they sold their home and they want to place the ashes next to our pets. They belong together, all three of them. Our two families will always be connected."

Marie kissed her husband and retreated to the house to spend more time with Lucky before it was time to put him to sleep. It was too painful for Marie to go to the vet; she left that duty to her husband and their son, Michael.

When it was time to go, Roxy retreated to a spot underneath the dining room table and watched as Thomas and Michael lifted up Lucky to carry him to the car. Michael sat in the back seat with Lucky on his lap.

"Dad, can you take a picture of us?" Michael asked. "I want to remember this day."

Michael handed over his cell phone and Thomas used it to snap a couple of photos before starting the car and backing out of the driveway. Lucky closed his eyes and fell asleep while Michael caressed him.

"Will Lucky and Lady be safe when we move away?" Michael asked.

"Yes, son. The new owners promised they will preserve the area. They have an urn with their dog's ashes that they will bury next to Lucky and Lady so all three dogs can be in peace."

"I want to write their names on the boulder so the new owners will know where our dogs are."

"That's a great idea, Michael. You can do that when we get home."

Thomas started daydreaming about one of his favorite movies, Marley & Me, starring Owen Wilson and Jennifer Aniston. He remembered how the family gathered together at the gravesite. It inspired him to do the same thing with his family when Lady was put to sleep. Now, it was time to repeat the ceremony one more time for Lucky.

Thomas looked in the rear view mirror and smiled when he saw his son gently petting Lucky. It was the first time he didn't see the caveman staring back at him. Thomas wondered if the caveman would stop haunting him once he and his family moved away.

"I feel Lady's presence," Michael said. "She knows Lucky is getting ready to be with her. Do you feel anything, dad?"

"Yes, son, I do. I've been feeling something for a while now. Lucky and Lady belong together. I'm really happy they will be in the place where they had so many great years together."

Thomas turned into the parking lot and found a space

in front of the vet hospital. Lucky woke up when Thomas turned off the engine and turned his head toward the window.

"Are you ready to see Lady?" Michael asked his pet, holding back tears.

Lucky didn't answer. His body was tired and he was ready to go sleep.

Thomas got out of the car and opened up the door for his son and Lucky.

"I think it's better if we carry him in," Thomas said.

"I can do it," Michael volunteered.

Thomas helped lift Lucky out of the back seat and grabbed a couple of sheets while Michael headed to the front door carrying Lucky like a newborn baby.

The vet was waiting at the reception area and opened the door to the exam room. She instructed Michael to lay Lucky on the cushion in the center of the room. She told Thomas and Michael it would be about ten minutes before she would return. She walked out and closed the door so Thomas and Michael could be alone with Lucky.

Thomas looked at his son as he was petting Lucky. He admired how loving his son was. There hadn't been much time to think about anything with the home on the market. Thomas savored the quiet moment and knelt down next to his son. "Lady is calling him, Michael. Lucky is ready."

There was a quiet knock on the door. The vet walked in and asked if was okay to start the procedure.

"Michael looked up and nodded his head."

The vet opened the cabinet and removed a shaver. "I'm going to give Lucky something so he wont' feel any pain," the vet said while shaving a small area on Lucky's paw. She gave him a shot of pain medicine and left the room.

Lucky became drowsy and closed his eyes. Ten minutes later, the vet returned. She explained the procedure and assured Thomas and Michael that Lucky would not feel any pain. She inserted the needle and injected the shot. A few minutes passed. Lucky's heart stopped. Thomas and Michael quietly wrapped Lucky in the sheets they brought with them and left the building. They drove home in silence. When they pulled into the driveway, they got out of the car and carried Lucky into the house. Roxy was at the front door waiting. She sniffed at the sheets and then followed Thomas and Michael out to the backyard. Marie was behind the group with a box of tissue. They walked over to the new grave site and placed Lucky in the hole. Marie watched while Thomas and Michael filled the hole with dirt.

When the hole was filled, Michael went inside and found a red marker. He rejoined the group and helped his dad put the boulder in place. Then, he wrote the words, R.I.P. Lucky, the best dog ever. He marked Lady's grave with the same words while his parents watched.

The winds gusted, knocking over several chairs that were outside.

"Their spirit will be with us forever," Thomas said.

"Rest in peace, Lucky and Lady," Marie added.

"The best dogs ever," Michael said. "Thank you, God, for letting them be with us and for letting them be together again. Please take good care of them until we see them again."

"You did a great job today, Michael," his father said. "Stay out here as long as you want. It's time for your mother and me to work on our packing. May God bless our dogs and the family who will be moving here soon."

Thomas looked at the date on his triathlon watch and raised his eyebrows before returning inside. The clock was ticking and it was almost time to get the moving truck. Thomas leaned down and placed his hand on Lucky's new headstone one last time. He paused for a moment and said, "Good-bye my friend, rest in peace."

Chapter Eight

"Thomas, will you and Marie please stand next to each other while we wrap this prayer quilt around you and pray?" Deacon Pat was an ex-firefighter who couldn't sit still. His official retirement lasted about thirty days. He became fidgety and decided to go back to school for a masters degree in theology. His desire to serve others trumped his plans to travel and see the world.

When Pat became a deacon one year earlier, it was Thomas who volunteered to host the welcoming party put on at the church. Friends contributed stories and photos for a slide show. Thomas shared how Pat put together a team of volunteers to feed the firefighters during the worst California firestorm in the state's history.

"Only Deacon Pat would go to K-Mart and buy a flashing light to put on his truck so he could get past the barricades and feed his friends," Thomas said at Deacon Pat's party. "Then, he found out where we were evacuated to and tracked us down so we could help him bring truckloads of food and water to the firefighters on the front lines who refused to leave their posts. Before we left base camp, Deacon Pat asked the captain for protective outer wear which included a blanket that looked like a giant roll of aluminum foil. He told our wives, 'don't worry, your husbands won't be anywhere near the flames,'" Thomas said, shaking his head no and raising his eyebrows.

"I was pretty sure when the flames encircled us that we were all going to turn into baked potatoes and and eventually someone would find us all wrapped up in tin foil," Thomas said while the crowd laughed.

"Do you remember when I told you guys, 'no media'"? Deacon Pat asked.

"And there you were, standing up on top of all the

supplies in the bed of my pickup truck when the cameras were rolling as we moved through the barricades to feed my buddies. And we ended up on live TV. You had to break the no media rule, didn't you?"

Thomas felt his wife squeezing him around the waist. The flash of the cameras from the crowd snapped Thomas out of his flashback moment about Deacon Pat's party. He looked out at the crowd and smiled while he and his wife were cuddled in their new prayer quilt.

"No media," Thomas joked, pointing his finger to Deacon Pat and pretending to hide behind the quilt.

Deacon Pat beckoned for the audience to come up and surround Thomas and Marie. When they got closer, they placed their hands on the quilt, crafted by a special group of ladies known as the prayers and squares committee. The ladies who made the quilt for the Morgan family as a going away gift prayed over each individual knot. The border displayed Bible verses in cursive about Faith, Hope and Love from Corinthians 13. The center of the quilt was filled with brilliant colored squares, mostly blue and turquoise.

Thomas and Marie bowed their heads while Deacon Pat led the closing prayer. When the prayer was done, Thomas spoke one last time.

"My friends, every time we wrap ourselves in this quilt on cold Winter nights in Iowa, we will remember the love you gave us. We will remember the prayers you sent us.

And we will never, ever forget you."

Bess grabbed Thomas and hugged him tightly. The ninety-two year-old was even feistier that Deacon Pat. "We will always be your angels, Thomas and Marie. And we will never forget you. When are you leaving?"

"We are loading up the moving truck tomorrow," Thomas said while using the quilt to wipe away his tears.

Marie closed out the party with her final words. "We love you. Thanks for the thoughtful gift. Good-bye."

Chapter Nine

The prayer quilt was one of the last items loaded onto the moving truck. It barely fit. The boxes were packed so tight they looked like they were part of a game of Tetris. Each one fit perfectly all the way to the roof. Two tons of "stuff" was left piled in the center of the garage. Roxy sniffed at the last remnants of the Morgans old life and pulled out one of her old toys. She shook the stuffed animal violently and stuffing spewed out from between the ears. Thomas knelt down and pulled the toy away.

"Sorry Roxy, you're friend can't go with us. He needs to stay with Lady and Lucky and guard the house. We'll find you a new friend when we get to Iowa."

Michael walked into the garage and asked, "Dad, is it okay if we bury this toy with our dogs?"

"That's a great idea, son. We'll be leaving in a few minutes. Can you ask your mother if she can join us in the backyard?"

"What about all this stuff in the garage, dad?"

"Our friends will be coming by tomorrow with a trailer. They'll sort out anything that can be donated. Everything else is going to the dump."

Thomas looked at the pile one last time before joining his family in the backyard. There was a collection of roller blades from when his children were younger. There were scooters with missing parts that the children refused to let go of. Thomas admired all the kitchen cabinets lining the walls of the garage. His brother-in-law helped him install the cabinets from the original kitchen when he remodeled his home.

I hope the new owners cherish this home as much as we did, Thomas thought as he closed the garage door for the last time before walking out to the backyard.

Michael, Marie and Roxy were all sitting next to the pet cemetery when Thomas approached. He pulled out his cell phone camera to take a picture.

"This better not be on Facebook," Marie cautioned Thomas.

"Don't worry, honey. Wilson, Ramona and Umbro are my only friends you're gonna see on Facebook. Smile, please."

"What are you talking about, dad?" Michael asked.

"I wanted to keep a journal of our move to Iowa and post stories on my Facebook page but your mom made me promise -- no family pictures."

"Who is Umbro?" Michael asked.

"I found him in the garage this morning. He is the soccer ball we won in a raffle. All the players from the San Diego Soccers autographed him. I named him 'Umbro' because that's what's on the label. He's from Pakistan."

"You're so weird, dad."

Marie laughed and put her hand over her mouth.

"You can blame your mother, Michael. She's the one

who made me promise there would be no family pictures online. Look at this."

Thomas opened up the gallery on his cell phone and showed off a picture of his tennis racket cover. "That's Wilson from the deck of our master bedroom. You can see the boulders we put on Lucky and Lady's graves in the background."

Thomas looked at his watch. "It's time to go. Can we get a picture?"

Marie chimed in, "I don't see your other friends. Where are they?"

"Ramona is getting a new string job at the club. She should be ready any time now. Wilson and 'Bro' are in the front seat."

"This is going to be a long road trip, isn't it?" Michael said while looking at his mother. "I think dad's going crazy."

Thomas thought of the caveman in the mirror. He wondered if the caveman was going to stay behind or join his inanimate friends in the moving truck.

"I think you're right, Michael," Marie said. "You're dad has been acting really strange lately. I hope his new friends keep him company. I think it will be good for your dad to keep a journal. Maybe if he writes more he'll get all his crazy thoughts out of his mind and he won't be so obsessive compulsive all the time."

Thomas snapped a few pictures and then the family headed back inside the house for a last-minute inspection. Thomas avoided looking at any mirrors while the family walked through their home for the last time. There was a strange echo from the empty walls and floors. Roxy seemed disoriented and stayed close to the family, not wanting to be left behind.

The doorbell rang and Roxy started barking uncontrollably. Michael picked her up and Marie opened the door.

"Hello, Amber. Your just in time," Marie said "We're about ready."

"Everything is set for the closing. I'll keep the keys until everything is finalized. My husband will be sending you the documents for signatures."

Marie handed over the keys. "Be sure to thank your husband for taking all our stuff to the dump. I'm so embarrassed."

"You're brother-in-law volunteered to help. A couple of trips to the dump and everything will be fine."

Amber watched as the family got inside the moving truck. "Can I take a picture?" Amber asked.

The moving truck was parked in the middle of the

street to accommodate the trailer towing the Ford Focus, still displaying stickers from Thomas' publishing business on the door panels. The inside of the car was packed so heavily that the tires looked like they were deflated. Neighbors were waving good-bye. Wilson and Umbro were propped up in the front windshield. Michael squeezed in between his parents and held Roxy in his arms.

Thomas started the engine and it rumbled. The Morgans flashed a "thumbs up" sign and Amber shot the picture and waved good-bye.

Chapter Ten

"Did you pack Ramona?" Thomas asked Marie as he approached the first stop sign at the end of the cul-de-sac.

"Sorry, Thomas. Her string job took longer than expected. We'll have to leave her at your sister's house until you can come back for her.

* * *

Michael turned and faced his mother. He asked, "mom, what are you doing calling dad's racket a 'she'? She's an *it*."

"You can blame dad. He treats her like part of the family. I think he spent too much time in the sun all those years on the tennis courts. He's having trouble separating the real from the inanimate."

The budget rental truck drove like a tank with all the extra weight from the trailer. Thomas had trouble coming to a complete stop at the bottom of the hill. He glanced in the driver's mirror and gave it a quick adjustment and then gave Wilson a pat, proud that was able to stop in time.

"Hang in there, Wilson. You're bride will be back with you soon."

Marie looked out the window and started daydreaming about what was ahead. The rental truck picked up speed once they left their hometown and began their descent from 1,500 ft. Thomas kept pumping the brakes to keep the speed below 45 mph. The first traffic light displayed a green right turn arrow but the vehicle was going too fast to make the turn. Thomas yelled, "hold on everybody!" He kept pumping the brakes but couldn't slow down. He ran the red light, narrowly missing a vehicle that was turning in front of him.

Marie screamed. Michael put his hands over his eyes

and froze. Several drivers that were stopped at the intersection honked their horns while the Morgans zoomed by.

Michael opened his eyes. Umbro, the soccer ball, was still on top of the dash board directly in front of Michael and appeared to be smiling.

"Is everyone okay?" Thomas asked, still pumping the brakes.

"That was a close call," Marie said, trying to catch her breath. "My whole life just flashed before my eyes."

Thomas finally got control of the moving truck and pulled over to the side of the road.

"Thank God we're okay," Thomas said. "I need to go a lot slower on those steep hills. We are carrying a lot of weight. There's no way I can make a U-turn here. Looks like we have our first detour."

"Thomas, this is a sign. I'm afraid. Did you see the weather report? There's a snow storm expected in Utah. Will you please re-route us on the southern route through Arizona? I don't want us to get stuck in a blizzard. We haven't even gone ten miles and you almost killed us."

Thomas sighed. "I really wanted you to see the beauty of Colorado and Utah, Marie."

Michael chimed in, "Yeah dad, but how can we see it if

we're dead."

Thomas looked in the mirror and checked for traffic before pulling out.

"We're not going to die. We have an amazing journey ahead. We have a new life. Okay, honey, we'll go with the alternate route. We can see Grandma when we pass through Arizona. Then we'll travel through New Mexico and Texas. I'll take you to Colorado and Utah for a family vacation."

Roxy started wagging her tail in approval from inside her travel carrier and the thumping noise got the family's attention. She seemed to be aware of the dangers ahead and perhaps sensed peace in Marie's tone of voice.

"Maybe dad's not that crazy after all," Marie said.

"Marie, do you remember when you and Michael kept telling me how you were hearing strange noised at night in our home?"

"That house is haunted, Thomas," Marie said.

"Yeah, dad. Just because you never heard anything doesn't mean it's not haunted."

"I didn't want to scare you but I did see something -- more than once."

"Aha! We were right, mom."

* * *

"What did you see, honey?" Marie asked.

"Something in the bathroom mirror."

"What kind of something?" Marie prodded.

"A man. He was shackled in chains and he wasn't wearing any clothes."

"He was in our house?" Michael asked.

"He was in the mirror."

"What was he doing?" Marie asked.

"He had a blank stare on his face. He looked kind of freaky, like he was on drugs."

"Why didn't you ever tell us?" Michael asked.

"I knew you two were already complaining about the house being haunted and I didn't want to worry you. We all have enough stress already with selling our home and moving out of California. We barely have enough money to get there and we don't have jobs."

"Dad, this is a big deal. What do you think the man wants?"

"I'm not sure. He looks lost."

* * *

"So, you saw him more than once?" Marie asked.

"He showed up a couple more times before the home sold. Something happened to him. His chains were gone the second time I saw him and he was wearing a robe. I could tell by the expression on his face that he was sad."

"Do you need to see a doctor?" Marie asked.

"Marie, I know you think I'm crazy because I have a bunch of friends traveling with us who aren't human. They are there for your protection. I'm keeping a journal about our trip and someday I might share my story with others. There will be lots of photos. I already promised you and Michael, no pictures of you two. I need my friends to pose in the pictures at all the places we visit. I'm not crazy. The man in the mirror is real. If I see him again, it means he's not haunting our house, he's haunting me. I feel like I have to find out who he is and why he's reaching out to me."

"When we get to Iowa, I'm making an appointment for you to see a doctor."

"Because I'm seeing things? What about you and Michael? You're hearing things. Besides, we don't even have insurance. How are we going to pay for the doctor visit?"

Michael interrupted. "Dad, if you see this man again, are you going to tell us?"

* * *

"Do you want to know?"

"Thomas, stop it. Why do you always have to answer a question with a question? Of course we want to know. Are we in danger?"

"Yes. I will tell you if I see him again. Maybe it was the house. Actually, the only thing haunting me was our bank. If they had been more cooperative, we could have been out of here a year ago, long before I saw the man in the mirror."

"Look. It's time to get on the freeway."

"Thomas, if you don't want anyone in Iowa to think you're weird, you have to stop calling it a freeway. They call them interstates back there."

Thomas turned on the turn signal. "Interstate ahead. Wilson and Bro, Are you ready?"

Chapter Eleven

Thomas parked the moving truck in an open area of the university parking lot, the first official stop on the journey. Teresa was already waiting with a packed suitcase.

Marie was the first to greet her.

* * *

"How are you, my daughter?" Marie asked, wrapping her arms around Teresa.

"Sorry were so late, Teresa," Thomas said while hugging her. "This truck moves really slow on the hills."

"You should see dad at the gas stations, Teresa," Michael laughed while covering his mouth. "He almost took out a gas pump at our last stop."

"Is anyone hungry?" Thomas asked, changing the subject.

Everyone nodded yes. "My next class is in an hour. Let's hurry," Teresa said, pointing to the school cafeteria. "Thanks for taking this suitcase."

Thomas opened up the back of the truck and shoved the suitcase into the last tiny space. Then, the Morgans headed off for lunch.

"Did you hear about dad's new friend?" Michael asked his sister while walking to the cafeteria.

Marie pressed her lips together and stared at Michael.

"What are you talking about?" Teresa asked.

"Yeah. Dad has a new friend. He lives in the mirror."

"I wouldn't call him a friend," Thomas said. "I'm not

really sure who he is."

"We just found out about him today, Teresa," Marie said. "Dad has been seeing him in our bathroom mirror."

"All this time dad's been criticizing us about the noises we've been hearing in the middle of the night. We tried telling him our house was haunted. And he never told us about his visions," Michael said.

"It doesn't matter. The house is sold and we're moving on," Thomas said.

Michael got up and picked up the carrier holding Roxy. "I'm going to take her for a walk before we need to leave."

Teresa looked at her watch. "Sorry guys, I need to get to class. Dad, let me know if you have any more visions. I'll be praying for all of you to have a safe trip. I'll be seeing you in a couple of months when school's out."

The Morgans exchanged hugs and Teresa led them out of the cafeteria. Marie held back tears as she watched her daughter depart. Thomas and Marie joined Michael and Roxy and headed back to the parking lot. Several cars parked beside the moving truck, making it difficult to exit. The parking lot resembled a drive-in movie theater with rolling mounds separating the rows of cars. As Thomas drove over the first mound, the trailer hitch touched the ground and began grinding. Marie jumped out to see what was causing the noise.

* * *

"We're stuck, Thomas. You need to look at this."

Thomas got out and began cursing when he saw the predicament.

"We're at a christian school, honey. Stop it," Marie urged.

"If that hitch unhooks, we're going to be here all night, Marie. This is one big mess. I'm going to back up. Make sure I don't hit anything."

The whole family was on edge as Thomas slowly moved the truck, inches at a time, carefully maneuvering past the parked cars and the uneven slopes. One hour later, the Morgans were finally free.

"Are you okay, Bro and Wilson?" Thomas asked while looking at the dashboard.

"I think they're sleeping," Michael said.

The family was packed in tightly and there was no room to stretch. Michael had his legs straddled around some items that were on the floorboard as he sat in between his mom and dad. Roxy was in her kennel on the floor next to Marie's feet.

"I don't think any of us will be able to sleep while we're driving," Marie said. "How far to the hotel?"

* * *

"I don't want to get a hotel until we're out of California. As soon as we get to Arizona, the prices will be lower. We've got three hours to go."

Marie and Michael tilted their heads toward each other and managed to fall asleep. Thomas used the quiet time to calculate the miles per gallon in his head and figure out how long the trip was going to take. He wasn't sure how he would hold up driving the entire distance himself but he couldn't afford the extra insurance to add Marie as a driver. Towing a vehicle made the drive difficult and Marie preferred to sit in the passenger seat.

"Eleven miles to the gallon, Wilson. I sure hope we have enough money to get to Iowa," Thomas said to his buddy on the dashboard.

"Hey Bro, take a look out the mirror at that sunset. Isn't it beautiful? That's the last California sunset we're gonna see."

Thomas reached over and turned the soccer ball 90° so it appeared Bro was looking out the driver's mirror. A thin layer of clouds stretched across the sky. Once the sun dipped below the horizon, the clouds turned red and purple. Thomas turned on the headlights. A large road sign came into view with the words, "Welcome to Arizona."

Thomas looked in the mirror and said, "Good-bye, California. It was nice knowing you. I'm going to miss you."

Chapter Twelve

"Hello, mom. It's Thomas. We're an hour outside Phoenix. Would you like to meet for lunch?"

Doris paused before answering. "I thought you kids were going through Utah and Colorado. This is a big surprise. I'm getting ready to meet my girl friends for bunco later on but I can take a break and make lunch at my house for your family. Do you want to stop by? You can see my latest re-decorating project."

Doris lived in the same house where she raised six children and she was proud of all the remodeling she did herself since retiring. Thomas grew up in the Sunnyslope area of North Phoenix. His dad purchased the home without ever showing his mother. It was a surprise she didn't appreciate and the home was too small for the growing family. After the divorce, Doris struggled to keep up with the repairs. Now that she was retired, she finally got the opportunity to make improvements that fit her taste. She hoped her children would come back home with their own children for summer vacations at grandma's.

"Sorry mom. We have a storm chasing us from the southwest and we need to stay ahead of it. How about we meet at the north end of town for a quick lunch?" Thomas asked.

"There's a new Mexican food restaurant in the strip center located right off the Loop 101 near Bell Road. Do you want to meet there?"

Thomas did a quick calculation in his head. I'm dying for Mexican food. We can be there is fifty-five minutes. You can't miss us. We're in a Budget moving truck and we're towing our car on a trailer. See you soon. Love you."

* * *

Thomas hung up his cell phone and hit the chronograph button on his triathlon watch.

"I'm so happy we get to see your mother, Thomas," Marie said.

"She's got a busy day planned with her bunco ladies. We're lucky we get to see her today. She wanted us to stop by and see the latest changes to her home but the storm is too close and we can't lose any time," Thomas said.

Thomas found the strip center and drove into the back corner of the parking lot. His mother was waving her arms to get his attention. Thomas glanced at his watch. "Fifty-five minutes exactly," he declared." Marie and Michael focused their attention on Doris. She donned a smile from ear to ear and couldn't wait to be re-united. Marie and Michael got out first and were the first to greet Doris. Thomas was busy gathering his soccer ball and his tennis racket cover before catching up to greet his mother.

"I thought you guys were in a hurry," Doris said while wrapping her arms around her family. "What's up with the tennis racket and the soccer ball?"

"You don't want to know, grandma," Michael said. "Dad's crazy. Those are his 'friends.'"

Marie rolled her eyes and nodded in agreement.

"What do you mean, crazy?" Doris asked Marie as the

foursome walked up to the restaurant.

Thomas interrupted the conversation and handed the soccer ball to Doris. He pulled out his cell phone camera. "Mom, this is Umbro. He's from Pakistan. We call him Bro. The family won't let me take any pictures of them so Bro and Wilson are in all the shots."

"That's because everything ends up on Facebook," Marie added.

Doris handed the soccer ball back to Thomas. "I hate the internet. Sorry, son. I don't want to be in any of these pictures either."

Thomas placed Bro next to Wilson at an outside table and shot a picture of his buddies while his mother stared at him.

"Grandma, I think you need to have a talk with dad. He's been really strange lately."

"What do you mean, Michael?"

"He's seeing things."

"What kind of things?"

The waitress came over to the table and saved Thomas from the embarrassment. "May I take your order?"

"Margarita, please," Marie said.

* * *

The waitress scribbled the orders and walked away. Doris turned back to Michael and asked, "what kind of things is your father seeing?"

"Dad says he's some kind of caveman."

Thomas interjected, "if you really want to know, mom, he looks like Charlton Heston from the Planet of the Apes, except he's on drugs. And by the way, I'm not the only one who is crazy. Marie and Michael have been hearing things for years."

Marie jumped in. "Doris, that house is haunted. Thomas is in denial. Michael and I heard noises in the middle of the night. Your son never believed us."

"It doesn't matter now, Marie," Thomas said. "The house is sold and we're out of California forever."

Doris asked, "can you tell me more about the caveman?"

Marie said, "the caveman is part of your son's vivid imagination. He's been under a lot of stress with our short sale and our move to Iowa. Anyone in his position would be seeing things, too."

"Maybe she's right, mom. I think I am a little bit crazy. Who in their right mind would move to a new place with no money and no job?"

"I will be praying for you," Doris said. She was a woman of faith. Despite her many trials, she refused to give up. "Remember, everything is in God's hands," she said.

The waitress dropped off the food and Marie sipped on her margarita. Doris looked at her son with his head down and tried to cheer him up. "Thomas, do you want to take a picture of me and Wilson together? Just promise me this won't end up all over the internet. Marie and Michael gathered behind Doris. Michael asked, "dad, can you toss Bro to me? This will be a great family picture. The waitress returned with the bill and asked Thomas if she could snap a picture. Thomas joined his family and looked down at the soccer ball. "Smile, Bro," he said as the waitress took the picture.

The family walked back to the moving truck and kissed each other good-bye. Doris had tears in her eyes as she watched the family climb into the truck. "Good-bye Thomas. Good-bye Marie. Good-bye Michael. Good-bye Wilson. Good-bye Bro."

Thomas waved Wilson in the air before putting him back on the dashboard with Bro and then blew his mother a kiss. "I love you," he said before driving off.

Chapter Thirteen

"This is unbelievable," Thomas said while banging on the steering wheel. "Any slower and we may need to cut a hole out underneath so we can use our feet to help climb these mountains."

"Just don't break the steering wheel, Bam Bam," Marie

said with a chuckle.

"Who's Bam Bam?" Michael asked.

"He was a cartoon character from the Flintstones, back in the day when your mom and dad were growing up."

"Yabba dabba do," Thomas hollered.

"Fred, you better stop it," Marie cautioned.

"Hey, Wilma, why don't you and Bam-Bam jump out and help push? That line of cars backed up behind us will really appreciate it."

As they were speaking, Michael read a text message from his sister.

"Teresa wants to know why you're going so slow. She said we should already be in Texas," Michael said.

"You can tell her we're going as fast as we can," Thomas said. "At least we have a tailwind."

The Morgans were sputtering at 20 mph up the steep climb on the Black Canyon Freeway. Thomas shifted into the lowest gear, causing the engine to shrill. The Morgans could barely hear one another speaking. The loud winds added to the noise. By nightfall, they made it to Flagstaff, a college town where Phoenicians travel to in the summer to avoid the oven in the valley of the sun where summer temperatures reach 120+°.

* * *

"Dad, it's getting really cold out. Do you think we can roll the windows up?" Michael asked.

"Hey, look. There's snow on the ground," Marie said.

"We're going to be seeing a lot more of that soon," Thomas added.

Two deer appeared out of nowhere and zipped in front of the truck. Thomas hit the brakes and narrowly missed them. Before he could say anything, a dozen more deer lined the side of the highway, frozen like statues.

"That was close," Thomas said, wiping his forehead. "I have to be really careful on these icy roads. I don't have much control."

The skies darkened as the sun set behind the mountains and snow flurries began to stick on the windshield.

"It's time for us to call it a night, honey," Thomas said to his wife. "Be on the lookout for a place to stay."

"That hotel over there has free internet," Michael said, pointing across the street.

Thomas pulled in and parked the truck outside the hotel lobby. A blast of cold air rushed in when he opened the door and Roxy cowered under her blanket. Michael coaxed her out and placed her in the snow. She sniffed around before doing her business and darted back to the truck.

Thomas yelled for his family to join him as he headed to their room.

"We're all set," Thomas said as he unlocked the door. "Let's get to bed early. They're expecting a big snow storm tomorrow and we need to get on the road early. I just found out some tornadoes touched down in Oklahoma. It might get a little scary soon."

Chapter Fourteen

Marie was the first one up. She reached over to the nightstand, grabbed the remote and turned on the news. The scenes of tornadoes touching down in Kansas and Oklahoma frightened her. "Thomas, wake up," she said, nudging Thomas from a deep sleep.

***

"What's wrong, mom?" Michael asked, peering out from his double bed a few feet away.

"There's some bad weather ahead," Marie said, this time shaking Thomas.

Thomas opened his eyes and looked at Marie. He saw the look on her face and knew something was wrong. Michael walked over to the hotel window and pulled back the curtains. "Look at all that snow," he said.

The local news reporter announced that a severe snow storm was rolling in by mid-day. He was broadcasting from a split screen. While he was talking, the news station was showing pictures of all the damage from the tornadoes that touched down the day before.

"We don't have much time, Marie," Thomas said. "We need to get on the road right away. Michael, can you please take care of Roxy? She's needs to go to the bathroom. When she's done, head over to the lobby and get yourself some breakfast."

Marie checked her cell phone and got a text from Amber in California. "They sent us the closing papers by email, Thomas. We need to sign everything right away and send them back electronically so they can close escrow."

"When it rains it pours," Thomas said.

"What about the tornadoes, dad?" Michael asked.

* * *

"They're a few states away, son. We don't have time to think about that right now. The most important thing for us to do is get on the road so we can miss the blizzard that's moving into the area. Marie, I'll work on the documents while you eat breakfast with Michael in the lobby."

Michael stared at the TV. Entire neighborhoods were flattened. Survivors in Oklahoma and Kansas were sharing their experiences. The devastation was horrific. Thomas reached for the remote and turned the TV off.

"Roxy needs you, Michael. Don't worry. We're going to be okay. Make sure you put your coat on before you go outside."

Michael zipped up his winter coat and placed the leash on Roxy before opening the door. The winds were swirling and Roxy refused to go outside. Michael bent down and picked her up.

"Come on, girl, let's go." The six pound chihuahua was shivering. She hid her face inside Michael's arms as he carried her across the parking lot. Thomas walked over to the corner of the room to get his laptop out of the suitcase. He stopped in front of the mirror and the wall and stared.

"Where are you?" He asked, searching for the caveman. All he could see was his own scruffy face. There were dark circles under his eyes and his hair was a mess. Marie walked up behind him and rubbed his shoulders. Thomas looked at her reflection and smiled.

"I don't know how you manage to look so good under these circumstances, Marie. I'm a mess and you look like you're going to a party."

"You're the one doing all the driving, Thomas. Michael and I get to sleep while we're on the road. Maybe you should have added me as a driver?"

"No way, Marie. You don't need to be driving that tank. Besides, the weather is going to get ugly. We need to get moving. If we get stuck in the blizzard, we could end up stuck here for days. We need to return the moving truck on time and we need to get to Iowa before we burn through all our cash."

"Okay, honey. We'll get some breakfast and check out. I'll send Amber a text and let her know you're sending the documents."

Michael knocked on the door and Marie let him in. His face was red and his clothes were covered in snow. As soon as he removed Roxy's leash, she jumped on the bed and disappeared under the covers. "Your just in time to join me for breakfast, Michael," Marie said, wrapping her scarf around her neck. "Dad will join us in a few minutes. Are you hungry?"

Marie and Michael went outside and headed for the lobby while Thomas located the email containing the closing documents. He found a checklist from Amber and a detailed set of instructions. At the end of the email, there were some kind words...

My husband and I are going to miss you. The whole town is going to miss you. Our thoughts are with you as you settle in your new community. Once we get your paperwork back, the mortgage company will send you a letter stating your debt is settled. You are finally free. Best wishes for success in Iowa.

Thomas wiped a tear from his eye. He thought of all the people he was leaving behind. Many felt trapped from the sudden down-turn in the economy. People were moving into tents because they had nowhere else to go. The short sale process took two years to finally complete due to all the stalling tactics from the mortgage company. Thomas read the email one more time before joining his family for breakfast. "We're free," Thomas said as he closed his laptop. "We're finally free."

Chapter Fifteen

Marie and Michael waited in the moving truck while Thomas scraped away a one inch layer of snow that accumulated on the windshield. Roxy was bundled up inside a ski jacket that the family was using as an extra blanket to keep warm. When Thomas finished, he opened the door and jumped in.

* * *

"Hurry, honey," Marie urged. "Get in. That wind is making us cold."

"Thanks for turning the heater on, Marie," Thomas said, buckling his seat belt. He checked the navigation on his cell phone and drove out of the parking lot.

"This is an important day for us," Thomas said. "The jet stream is bringing in more snow and it's right behind us. If we manage to stay ahead of it, we should be able to reach Texas by tonight. We'll spend the night there and then turn north. We'll be in tornado alley when we reach Oklahoma. The good news is we should be able to get through okay. Colorado and Utah are getting hit so hard they had to close the interstate we would have been on if you hadn't talked me into taking this route."

"You can be really thick-headed sometimes, Thomas," Marie said. "I'm glad you came to your senses. I just don't know about those tornadoes."

"One state at a time, Marie. One state at a time. Let's get through the rest of Arizona and all of New Mexico first. Oklahoma and Kansas are still far off. Right now we need to worry about the ice. Do you see that slush on the windshield? That means the temperature is right about 32° outside. The roads are going to be tricky. Let's hope it starts warming up."

Thomas pumped the brakes a couple of times to test the road. The white snow on the ground outside made everything look like a Christmas card.

"Hey mom and dad, look at that rainbow," Michael said, pointing in front of him. "It's a double rainbow."

"Picture time," Thomas said, pulling over and stopping on the pavement on the side of the highway.

Michael reached for Wilson and Bro and tossed both of them to his dad. "Have fun, dad," he said.

Thomas got out of the moving truck and walked over to a pine tree where he placed Wilson and Bro for a photo. The gusty winds knocked Wilson down. Thomas pulled his beanie over his ears and leaned down to pick him up. Marie and Michael watched from inside the moving truck. Marie rolled the window down and shouted, "Thomas, Bro is rolling away." Thomas turned toward Bro and started chasing after him. Marie and Michael were laughing the whole time.

"This reminds me of Chevy Chase when he wrecked the car in the middle of nowhere," Michael said to his mother. "It's too bad we're not recording this. Dad looks so silly." Bro was picking up speed on the downhill slope and Thomas was falling behind. Finally, Bro ran into a boulder and stopped. By the time Thomas reached Bro he was panting.

"Your dad is definitely a lot like Chevy Chase," Marie said to her son. "He doesn't try to be funny, he just is. Just be glad it's Wilson and Bro out there with your dad and not us."

Thomas reached down and picked up Bro and then climbed back up to retrieve his racket cover that was still laying in the snow. He propped Wilson up and placed Bro next him. "Smile guys," he said, pointing his cell phone camera to his inanimate friends for a few shots. He managed to take the pictures with the rainbow in the background before it disappeared when the clouds covered up the sun.

When Thomas got back inside, he placed his friends back on the dashboard and buckled up. Thomas looked at Michael and Marie. They remained silent. "What's that smirk on your faces?" Thomas asked.

"We were just wondering who was funnier, you or Chevy Chase," Marie said.

"Well, I know my family is much better looking than his family," Thomas said.

"And we don't have any dead bodies on top of the truck," Michael added.

"I don't think Bro and Wilson can be classified as living," Marie said.

"Are you kidding, honey?" Thomas asked. "Didn't you see how fast Bro was going down that slope?"

"Yeah, dad, Bro was kicking your butt out there."

***

The Morgans passed the time away by sharing memories from all the National Lampoon's Vacation movies. The heavy tail winds pushed them through Arizona and into New Mexico. They found a hotel near the New Mexico-Texas border and camped out for the night.

Thomas pulled in to the hotel parking lot and found an open area.

"We're at the half-way point," he said as he turned off the ignition.

"Way to go, Clark," Marie said. "Do we have time to stop at Wally World?"

"Sorry Ellen, they're still closed for repairs."

Michael watched his dad pick up Bro and Wilson from the dashboard and shook his head.

"Dad, are you sure you're not related to Chevy Chase?" Michael asked.

"Son, the closest thing we have to a movie star in this family is Wilson. His famous cousin played Wilson in the Tom Hanks movie, Cast Away. Sorry, Bro. I know you tried out for the part."

Thomas looked at his wife as they walked into the hotel lobby. "Ellen, do you think I hurt Bro's feelings about missing out on the movie gig?"

"You need some sleep, Clark. You're delirious."

Thomas set Bro and Wilson on the counter and said hello to the clerk.

"We would like to check in please. It's my wife and I, our son, Michael, our dog, Roxy, and we need a pullout bed for Wilson and Bro."

The clerk was speechless.

"If that's a problem, these two can sleep in the moving truck," Thomas said, pointing to his inanimate friends on the counter.

"No problem sir," the clerk responded. "But I need to put you in a special room for the dog and it will be an extra thirty bucks."

"And if you don't mind giving us a 5:00 AM wake-up call in the morning, that would be great. Do you know if Wally World is open?"

Marie grabbed Thomas by the arm. "Sorry about my husband," she said. "He gets silly when he's sleep deprived."

The Morgans headed up to their room and called it a day.

Chapter Sixteen

The phone rang at 5:00 AM. Thomas was already awake. He was sorting through his remaining cash cards given to him by his friends before he left California. The cards were inside three gift-wrapped tennis cans which also contained encouraging notes and treats for the road.

* * *

"What are you doing?" Marie asked.

"I'm making sure we have enough money and cash cards to get to Iowa," Thomas replied. "As long as we stick to Subway for our meals and we take advantage of the free breakfasts at the hotels, it looks like we should make it. We really need to get through tornado alley before any more tornadoes hit. It looks like it's going to be really windy the rest of the way. Good thing that tail wind is helping us with our gas. Do you think we can be on the road in an hour?"

"Yes, honey," Marie replied, nudging Michael from his deep sleep. Michael opened his eyes and sat up. "I just had a dream we were in a tornado. Our hotel room flew up in the air and landed in Kansas," Michael said.

"Well son, if we don't get on the road soon, we may end up in one later today. There's a reason they filmed the Wizard of Oz in Kansas. Tornadoes can happen at any moment and this is the season. We have to hustle. Why don't you and mom get dressed and let Roxy out and then head over to get breakfast? I'll meet you in the dining room as soon as I load up our bags."

Michael and Marie put a leash on Roxy and opened the door while Thomas got the bags together. A gust of wind whirled through their room, scattering the gift cards all over the floor. Thomas hustled to gather them up.

"It doesn't look like a good day to go to Wally World," Thomas said with a frown.

* * *

"Cheer up, Clark. We'll do that on our next vacation," Marie said.

"All right, Ellen," Thomas said, flashing his Chevy Chase smile.

Thomas loaded up their belongings in the moving truck and joined his family in the dining room. The other guests were glued to the TV.

"Stay off the roads today and tomorrow," the meteorologist warned. "Tornadoes are likely to occur without any warning."

The Morgans sat down facing the TV and the manager walked over to greet them.

"Which way are you headed?" he asked.

Thomas replied, "We're going through Texas, Oklahoma and Kansas today."

"You won't find too many on the highway where you're going, folks," the manager said. "It's getting dangerous out there. Are you sure you don't want to stay here a couple more days?"

"We have to get the moving truck back or we're going to have to pay extra," Thomas said.

Marie and Michael were staring at the video clips of the

tornado damage from the day before while the manager offered his advice about traveling in bad weather.

"Enjoy your complimentary breakfast," the manager said. "And be careful out there. If you don't have a weather app for your phone, you might want to download one. At least you will know where the bad weather is."

Thomas stuffed his coat pockets with an extra banana, orange and an apple before loading up his plate. Michael whispered in his mother's ear, "mom, I bet Chevy Chase does that on his vacations, too."

Marie whispered back, "son, dad already told me I'm in charge of the muffins. I'm loading up my pockets before we go."

Michael whispered back, "you and dad are criminals. I hope you don't go to jail."

The family sat down and ate quickly. When they were finished, they made their way back to the moving truck. The wind was blowing so hard that they could barely hear each other as they jogged through the parking lot. Roxy was staring out the window of the truck, barking nonstop. Thomas opened the door and spoke to her. "Are you ready to go to Kansas today, Toto? What about you guys, Bro and Wilson? Are you ready for some adventure today?"

The Morgans climbed in and buckled up. The dense clouds racing across the dawn sky made it hard to see.

Marie turned on a flashlight and opened up her Bible. "Listen to this," she said as she read from the 23rd Psalm, "Even though I walk through the darkest valley, I will fear no evil, for you are with me; your rod and your staff, they comfort me."

"Here's your staff right here," Thomas said, picking up Wilson from the dashboard and waving him in front of her.

"If you keep that up I'll be showing *you* the rod," Marie quipped.

"It better be an over-size rod," Thomas added. "We're crossing the border into Texas. Every thing's bigger in Texas."

Marie ignored her husband and kept reading to herself. Tumbleweeds danced across the road like an army advancing on the front lines. Thomas pulled over to the side of the road and asked Michael to join him as he reached over to pick up Wilson. "Bring Roxy's leash with you, son," Thomas said.

"What are you doing?" Marie asked.

"Just taking a quick break, honey," Thomas replied.

"Hurry up, Thomas," Marie said. "I don't like the way those clouds are looking. I'm scared."

Marie and Roxy watched from inside the truck as

Thomas strapped Roxy's leash onto Wilson. "Get a picture of this, Michael," Thomas said, letting out slack on the leash. Wilson was flapping in the wind about ten yards away while Michael snapped some pictures.

"Wilson!" Thomas yelled. "Wilson, come back!"

Marie couldn't believe what she was seeing. When Thomas and Michael were done reeling Wilson back in, Thomas pointed to a giant statue of a cowboy who had his gun drawn. "Pretend you're shooting at the cowboy," Thomas said, taking the camera from his son. "I'll take your picture." The thirty foot cowboy overshadowed Michael who was using Wilson as his rifle. "Okay, dad, you can take the picture. Just remember, if this ends up on FaceBook, I'm going to have to shoot you."

Marie rolled her window down and yelled, "Tornado!"

Thomas pointed his camera at the funnel cloud and snapped some pictures.

"Thomas!" Marie screamed, "Get over here!"

"Come on, Michael. Let's take cover in the truck." The two ran back to the truck and got inside.

"What are we going to do, Thomas?" Marie asked. "That tornado is headed right at us."

Thomas was out of breath. He fumbled with the keys before starting the engine. "We're going to get the hell out of here, that's what we're going to do." Thomas pressed the accelerator to the floor. The engine squealed.

"It's getting closer," Marie hollered, clutching her Bible. Hundreds of tumbleweeds smashed into the moving truck as the Morgans headed north. The funnel cloud touched down behind them within a hundred yards of the oversize cowboy, ripping him off of his foundation. He disappeared into funnel cloud. Michael watched the whole thing from the passenger window.

"Dad, the cowboy's gone," Michael yelled. Marie closed her eyes. Rain pelted the windshield. Thomas turned the wipers on to full speed and leaned forward. "I wish this truck could go faster," he said. A tree branch split off and flew across the highway in front of the Morgans. Marie pulled her prayer quilt over her and Michael and she cried out, "Dear God, please get us through this."

Thomas kept driving. Their moving truck was the only vehicle on the Texas highway. He reached for his phone and handed it to his son.

"Michael, I need you to find me a weather app. I want to know what's ahead. That tornado was a close call."

Michael used his two thumbs to search for the weather app. "Sorry dad, there's no reception out here."

"Well, it looks like were on our own," Thomas said.

***

Marie pulled down her prayer quilt and opened her Bible again to Psalms. She repeated, "Even though I walk through the darkest valley, I will fear no evil, for you are with me; your rod and your staff, they comfort me."

Thomas said, "you're right, Marie, God is with us -- you, me and Michael."

Roxy appeared from under the blanket for the first time and whimpered. Thomas looked at her and corrected himself, "you, me, Michael...and Toto."

Chapter Seventeen

"We're flying blind, Marie," Thomas said. "I can't see a thing out there." The rain was coming down in buckets. Broken pieces of tumbleweed were held captive on the wiper blades like prisoners of war in Mother Nature's battle. Their screeching voices were like fingernails on a chalk board.

* * *

"Can we pull over?" Marie asked.

"Sorry honey. We're not safe here. We have to keep moving," Thomas responded. Even at full speed, the wipers were no match against the rain. Thomas leaned forward and squinted his eyes for a better look through the fogged up windshield. The tumbleweeds maintained their assault. Michael closed his eyes and tried to sleep, his head bobbling every time the truck hit a pothole or ran over debris scattered on the deserted highway.

One hour passed before anyone talked about the near miss with the tornado. "Thomas, do you think that close call with the tornado is a sign from God?" Marie asked.

"Here's how I see it, Marie. We've been on the edge all our lives. I held your hand when you were in labor all those hours with the umbilical chord wrapped around Michael's head. Every time you had a contraction, his heart rate dropped. It scared the hell out of me. I felt so helpless. The doctor assured us everything would be okay. I prayed. And you delivered a healthy baby. You were at the end of your rope but you didn't give up. When I ran that red light at the beginning of our trip, we made it through the intersection unscathed. If we waited two extra minutes to video that tornado ripping the giant cowboy off his foundation we'd all be dead right now. But we're not dead. We're alive. This place is the shadow of death. I'm convinced God is with us right now just as He was when you were in labor for thirty-six hours. He's going to deliver us out of these shadows."

***

Mother Nature was listening for her cue. The moment Thomas finished talking, the rains stopped. The tumbleweeds halted dead in their tracks. The winds dissipated. A rainbow appeared in front of the Morgans. Michael opened his eyes and reached down to pick up Roxy from her kennel.

"Check it out, Roxy, it's a rainbow," Michael said.

Thomas looked over at Marie. "There's your sign from God, my love."

The next hundred miles was one long straight-away. Uprooted trees lined both sides of the highway. Thomas stopped for gas at the Texas-Oklahoma border and got out of the truck. "Anyone hungry?" Thomas asked.

Michael responded, "Subway?"

Marie chimed in, "I'm not sure I'll ever be able to eat at Subway again when this trip is over."

Thomas quipped, "Maybe we can set the world record for most Subway meals in a row?"

"No thanks, dad," Michael said. "I agree with mom. This is getting old."

"Welcome to Subway," the clerk said when the Morgans walked in. Marie and Michael shrugged their shoulders as they marched to the bathrooms. Thomas placed the order for his family and pulled out his gift card to pay.

"Where are you from?" the clerk asked.

"California."

"I bet those earthquakes are pretty scary."

"We never saw anything like the tornado that touched down on the side of the road earlier today," Thomas said.

"A whole town in Oklahoma got wiped out yesterday," the clerk said. "The tornado appeared without any warning. The elementary school was the hardest hit. Most of the kids never made it out."

"Don't say anything to my wife and son. They're still shook up and I don't want them to get too scared. We're on a deadline to get to Iowa and we have to keep moving no matter how bad the weather gets. I'm really glad you don't have any TV's in here. My son keeps having nightmares from all the tornado coverage."

Marie and Michael joined Thomas and sat down to eat. Michael led the prayers.

"Thank you, God, for watching over us on this trip. Thank you for rescuing us from the tornado. Please bless this food and keep us safe."

When they were finished eating, Marie checked her cell phone for messages.

* * *

"Teresa wants to know why we're still on the road with all the tornadoes in the area," Marie told her husband. "She's been trying to call us all day."

"Tell her we'll be safer once we get further north. Not even the hotels are safe here around here," Thomas said.

Michael nodded in agreement. "You're right, dad. Remember the dream I had about the tornado that hit our hotel room."

Marie responded to several text messages while Thomas and Michael cleaned up.

"Hurry along, Dorothy," Thomas said, motioning for his wife to join him. "We're on our way to Kansas."

"What about Oklahoma?" Michael asked.

"Yes, son. Oklahoma's first, but only the part just above the Texas panhandle. We'll be through it before you can blink. Don't forget to bring some extra water for Toto."

Oklahoma was eye-opening. The Oklahoma tornadoes were 24 hours ahead of the Morgans and they seemed to be following the same course the tornadoes were on. Downed power lines caused the highway to be closed the day before; road crews worked overtime to clean up the mess. The tail winds were gusting again. Ironically, the Subway sign was torn off the building at the next gas stop.

***

"I know both of you are really upset about missing out on our chance at a world record for the most meals eaten at Subway," Thomas told his family. "If you're willing to hang on for a while longer, how about some Kansas City barbecue?"

"Oh, I'm clicking my little red heels," Marie responded. "I'm closing my eyes and dreaming about a nice hot meal and a comfy bed tonight. Wake me up when we get to Kansas City."

Chapter Eighteen

"Wake up, Marie, we're here."

Marie opened her eyes. The sky was dark and the restaurant parking lot full. Thomas found an open area and parallel parked in front of the Kansas City Barbecue.

* * *

"We're in Kansas?" Marie asked.

"Missouri," Thomas replied. "You and Michael have been sleeping for hours. You both slept through an entire state. We're not in Kansas anymore, Dorothy. And this is our last night on the road. Tomorrow we'll be in Iowa."

Michael stretched out his arms and let out a big yawn. "No Subway tonight, dad?" he asked.

"This is our last supper on the road, Michael, and we're living it up. Let's go get something to eat."

Roxy was the last one to wake up. She scratched at the door to her travel carrier and let out a few barks. "You boys get us a table and I'll join you in a few minutes. I'll take care of Roxy," Marie said as she climbed out of the moving truck. The winds were still swirling.

Michael and Thomas walked across the parking lot and put their names in for a table. The smell of barbecue ribs filled the air. Thomas studied the menu at the counter while the two waited for Marie to join them. "I think I'm going with the Babybacks tonight, Michael," Thomas told his son. "Wow. I feel like I'm home here. There's a place just like this in San Diego. It was featured in the Top Gun movie. You're gonna love the food here."

Marie walked in and joined the family in time to be seated. She looked at the menu while Thomas chatted about their future. "By this time tomorrow, we'll be done with our road trip. I'm starting to get excited."

***

"Do we know where we're gonna be living yet?" Michael asked.

"There's a lot we have to do in the next thirty days," Thomas replied. "The first big step is to get jobs. Mom's friends are letting us stay in their home while they're on vacation. We'll be about an hour's drive from the town your mom wants to live in. If the job search goes well, I want to buy a home for us."

"Don't get your hopes up, Thomas," Marie said. "You know what Amber said about qualifying. That short sale is going to haunt us. Amber told us to wait three years. I'm okay with an apartment."

The waitress stopped by and introduced herself. "How are you'all doing tonight. My name is Sara. Tonight's special is Babyback Ribs with Cole Slaw, Potato Salad or BBQ Beans."

"Can I get french fries with my ribs?" Michael asked.

"You bet, sweetie."

Thomas asked his wife, "would you like to split the ribs for two?"

Marie nodded. "Do you have margaritas?" Marie asked Sara.

"Sorry, honey," she responded.

* * *

"Make it a Budweiser for me," Thomas said.

"Make it two," Marie added.

"How about some delicious corn on the cob to go with your supper?" Sara asked.

"No thanks," Thomas replied. "We'll be eating lots of corn where we're going."

Sara departed and the Morgans returned to their conversation.

"I know what Amber said about our credit," Thomas said to his wife. "But I believe we can get seller financing and we will find a nice place to buy."

"Let's at least get jobs first, Thomas," Marie urged.

"Let's not forget about Roxy," Thomas said. "There aren't many apartment places that will accept pets."

"You're dreaming again, Thomas," Marie said.

"I'm glad dad's dreaming," Michael added.

"Right now, I'm dreaming about those ribs," Thomas said. "I'm starving."

Sara returned to the table and served their meal.

* * *

"Here's your supper," Sara said.

After she walked away, Thomas leaned over and told his wife, "I don't remember anyone calling my dinner supper."

"Get used to it Thomas. Iowans eat dinner at lunchtime and supper in the evening. And don't expect anyone to sell us a house when we don't have jobs or credit."

"One thing I promise you, Marie," Thomas said. "I'm going to hit the ground running. I'll be out there every day looking for a new job and for a place we can own. And every night I'll be home in time for supper."

Marie and Michael shook their heads. "I think you married a crazy man," Michael said to his mother. "Was dad always like this?"

"Oh yes, Michael. That's one of the reasons I love him so much. He's always had a crazy side to him. I can't wait to find out what the people in Iowa think of him."

Chapter Nineteen

"That's it," Thomas declared to his wife. "That's the last tank of gas we need to get home." Michael gave a thumbs up while wiping all the bugs from the windshield.

"Thank God," Marie responded. "I don't think I can take another day in this moving truck. I'm ready to be home."

Marie's cell phone was beeping steadily. Marie rolled down her window and poked her head outside. "Great news, Thomas. My sister found us a storage place for all our stuff and she organized a group to help us unload everything. They want to know when we will be arriving."

Thomas put the gas cap back on and waited for the receipt before returning to the moving truck. The winds were gusting and he had trouble hearing Marie. "Sorry honey," he said once he was back in the driver's seat, "I could barely hear you out there. What's up?"

"We have a storage place for our stuff and my siblings can meet us to unload the truck. They want to know when they should show up."

"That's awesome," Thomas said. "The moving truck is due back tomorrow morning. We can be there in two hours. Let's have everyone meet us at the storage place to unload everything."

Marie's cell phone beeped again. Marie raised her arms up in the air and yelled, "woo-hoo, Fred and Stacey left the keys to their home under the door mat for us. They won't be home for at least six weeks. They want us to eat all the food in the refrigerator. Can you believe it?"

"Everything is happening so fast," Thomas replied. "I'm feeling really good about this. How far away is their home?"

"It's about an hour from the storage place," Marie answered. "By the way, Kathleen wants us to have supper with them tonight and spend the night. What should I tell my sister?"

Thomas paused for a moment before answering. His head was spinning.

"Perfect," he replied. "We'll meet your siblings to unload, drive over to Kathleen's for supper, spend the night, and then first thing in the morning, we can all drop off the moving truck and get settled at Fred and Stacey's place."

"One more thing, honey," Marie said. "Tomorrow is St. Patrick's Day and there's a party everyone's going to. Do you think we can go?"

"Can I bring Wilson and Bro?" Thomas asked.

Michael shook his head no. "Dad, they're going to think you're weird. Can't you just be normal?"

Thomas looked at his friends on the dashboard. He asked his son, "Michael, remember why Bro and Wilson are with us? You and mom refuse to be in the pictures so I need my buddies for all my Facebook posts. I'll tell you what, Wilson can go with us and I'll leave Bro at home. Besides, Bro is from Pakistan and they don't celebrate St. Patrick's Day in the Middle East. Wilson, he's Irish and he needs to be mingling with his Irish friends. Are you all right with that?"

"If it's okay with you, dad, I would rather stay home and take care of Roxy and Bro while you, mom and Wilson go to the party. I'm pretty wiped out from this trip."

"Wilson can wear my green beads," Marie said. "I think he'll be the life of the party."

"At least he won't object to being photographed," Thomas said.

"You seem awfully giddy, Marie," Thomas surmised. "When this trip started you wanted nothing to do with Wilson and Bro."

"I'm just getting really excited to be re-united with my family. And these two guys are helping us to enjoy our road trip. Just look at us, we're all calling them by their names now. Maybe you're rubbing off on us, Thomas."

"Maybe Wilson and Bro are rubbing off on you," Thomas replied. "It's just too bad they can't help us with the unpacking."

"Don't worry, Thomas, all my relatives will be there and there will be plenty of hands to help us with the unpacking."

Marie's face glowed like an angel when she spoke about

her family. She could barely contain herself as she watched the mile markers on the interstate, each one reminding her of distant memories from her youth.

"Are we there yet?" Michael asked his mother.

"Almost," Marie replied. "Almost."

Chapter Twenty

The cars were lined up at the storage lot like a funeral procession when Thomas rolled in. Marie's siblings, nephews and nieces were already in formation to unload the moving truck. Marie jumped out before Thomas came to a complete stop and got mobbed by her family. Roxy panicked from the commotion and tried to break out of her carrier. Michael restrained her but she wouldn't stop barking.

The men got to work on the trailer and unloaded the Morgan's passenger car within five minutes before unhitching the trailer from the moving truck. Thomas rolled the door open and pulled out the ramp. Twenty minutes later the truck was empty.

"It took two days to pack this truck," Thomas said, looking astonished.

"I can't believe we're here," Marie said. "It's so wonderful to be with all of you."

Karla was the first of the sisters to speak. "Before you arrived we were all fighting about who would get to host you and I'm the winner. We wanted to do a barbecue tonight but there's a storm coming and we decided to do the welcome home party indoors. Come on. Let's celebrate."

"Let's all huddle up first," Marie's only brother, Nathan said, motioning for everyone to get closer. "I would like to offer a prayer of thanks."

The winds were blowing hard and the rain clouds were rolling in. Michael removed his San Diego Chargers cap and placed it over Roxy to keep her calm.

"Do you mind if I get a picture of this?" Thomas asked. He opened the door to the moving truck and climbed in to retrieve Wilson and Bro from the dash board.

"Oh no," Marie said under her breath.

Marie's sisters seemed puzzled when they saw the tennis racket cover and the soccer ball.

"This is the rest of the family," Thomas said, tossing Bro to Wendy, the youngest of Marie's sisters. "And this is Wilson. These two are in all our family pictures from the road trip." Thomas handed Wilson over to Julie, the quietest sister of the group. Julie started waving Wilson around like she was playing tennis.

Marie tried to restore order. "Hurry up, Thomas," she said. "It's going to start raining any minute and my brother wants to pray."

"Wendy, can you hold Bro up a little higher?" Thomas asked. "Perfect. Smile everybody." Thomas snapped a few pictures and then asked Nathan if he was ready.

"Please bow your heads," Nathan said. "Heavenly Father, thank you for watching over our sister and her family during their move to Iowa. Please lead them to new jobs and provide a nice place for them to live. Amen."

As soon as Nathan finished, it began to rain. Thomas got back in the truck and backed it up to the trailer while Nathan guided him. As soon as he was lined up, Nathan hooked the trailer back onto the hitch and re-connected the wiring for the brake lights. Marie and Michael started up the family car and pulled in behind Thomas. Julie and Wendy handed Wilson and Bro back to Thomas before getting in their cars.

"Party at Karla's," Karla shouted to the group. "Let's go."

Thomas tooted the horn and Karla led the procession out of the parking lot.

Chapter Twenty-one

Thomas looked into his driver's side mirror and smiled at his wife and son who were following him closely. "This is it, boys," he said to Wilson and Bro. "What do you guys think about this town?" The sound of the wiper blades was all that could be heard. Thomas looked around at his new surroundings. He noticed all the other drivers waving at him at the oncoming traffic passed by.

"Hey, Bro, are you getting a kick out of this?" he asked. "Look, Wilson. I'm calling this the Iowa wave. See. All you have to do is lift up a couple of fingers and throw in a head nod. Marie and Michael are going to be so proud of me."

Suddenly, Thomas pulled over to the side of the road and hit the brakes. The caravan in front of him stopped to see what was wrong. Marie pulled up beside him and Michael rolled down the window. "What's up, Thomas?" Marie asked. Thomas pointed to the street sign. "Check it out. It's Wilson Street. Michael, jump out and take a picture of me and Wilson in front of the sign." Marie's other siblings got out their cars and walked over in the rain to see what was going on.

"We're okay," Marie told her family members while shaking her head. "Thomas is just being Thomas. He couldn't wait for a sunny day to get a picture of Wilson on Wilson Street. He's certainly not thinking about how famished his wife and son are. No. He had to pull over in the rain and stop the whole caravan so he could snap a picture of his *friend*."

"Marie, we've made it 1,800 miles without a fight. We've got five miles to go. Can you please humor me and let me have a little fun?"

Michael pointed his cell phone camera at his dad and Wilson. "Make sure you see the street sign in the photo,

Michael," Thomas told his son. Michael snapped the photo and everyone returned to their vehicles.

"Don't worry, Mom," Michael told his mother. I don't think there are any streets named Bro."

"If you're dad's not careful, there may soon be a gravestone named Thomas," Marie told her son. "And Wilson and Bro can rest in peace with your dad for eternity."

Michael changed the subject. "Mom, it sure feels good to stretch my legs. That moving truck was too cramped." He put his seat back all the way and let out a big yawn.

"Don't go to sleep, yet, Michael," Marie told her son. "There's going to be lots of food at your Aunt Karla's house. Your cousin Denise is letting your dad and me sleep in her room tonight and you'll be sleeping on the couch after the party is over. This is going to be a great opportunity for you to get to know your cousins on my side of the family.

"How do you think dad will do here?" Michael asked.

"You're dad gets along great with others. My only concern is that the caveman who was haunting him in California follows him out here."

"What's the story with the caveman?"

* * *

"Your dad thinks maybe one of his relatives from a long time ago is haunting him. He was seeing him in the mirror. It all started when he was working on his ancestry project. You know how your dad gets. He obsesses over things."

"Mom, you and I both know our home in California was haunted. Dad was probably seeing ghosts."

"I don't know any ghosts who wear chains," Marie said.

"Maybe an outlaw ghost?" Michael asked.

"Your dad never believed our home was haunted. Just because he never noticed anything, he was sure *we* were the crazy ones. Then his caveman started showing up in our bedroom mirror and I told your dad we had to get out of there."

"Son, whatever you do, please don't go blabbing to all my family about dad's caveman. I'm hoping all our ghosts stay in California and we can have normal lives here in Iowa. As long as your dad and I can find jobs right away, we're going to be in great shape."

"And a place to live?" Michael asked.

"Don't worry, Michael. Our friends are letting us stay in their place until they come home from their Winter break in Arizona. And if we need more time to find jobs, we can stay with one of my sisters."

* * *

"And if our ghosts follow us?"

"Son, our home in California was built on a mountain that was once a sacred burial ground for the Indians. I think we will be in peace now that are off the mountain. There aren't any skeletons around here, just a lot of corn fields. Let's not talk about the ghosts in front of anyone, okay?"

"Deal."

Karla led the caravan to her home and parked in the driveway. The rest of the family parked on the country road in front of her home. The moving truck barely fit under the tree branches from the oak trees lining both sides of the road. Marie parked behind Thomas and walked up to greet him.

"Can you help me with our friends?" Thomas asked.

"Sorry, honey, they're your friends. Why don't you let them sleep in the truck while we get situated? Besides, I think we already have enough pictures of your friends to last a lifetime."

"Good night, guys," Thomas said to Wilson and Bro. "We'll see you in the morning." Thomas locked the door to the moving truck and his family went inside Karla's home for the welcome home party.

When everyone sat down to eat, Karla asked the Morgans, "do you have anything exciting to share about your lives in California? We want to know everything."

Michael glanced at his mother and noticed the look on her face. He answered, "Well, it's too bad Wilson and Bro can't talk because if they could they might have something juicy to share. As for the rest of us, our lives are pretty boring."

Chapter Twenty-two

"Come on, spill the beans," Karla prodded. "We're all family here. We want to know what it's like to live in California."

"We are more interested to know what it's like to live in Iowa," Thomas responded. "There are certain things we prefer to leave behind us."

"Like what?" Karla asked.

"Like the caveman," Thomas blurted.

"And the ghosts," Michael added.

Marie glared at her husband and her son. She wished they kept their mouths shut. It was too late.

"We lived in a haunted house," Michael said.

"Did you ever see them?" Michael's cousin asked.

Marie put her head down and kept eating. Michael's face lit up with enthusiasm as he shared the story about the ghosts.

"Mom and I heard them in the middle of the night. It was like they were walking in between the walls."

"Rodents," Thomas said. "You were hearing rodents."

"Yeah, right dad. Rodents who were dragging suitcases full of stuff in the middle of the night. Rodents who talked to each other. And rodents who turned on the kitchen appliances when we were all sleeping."

"But you never saw them, did you?" Thomas asked.

"What about you, dad? You saw the caveman. Why

don't you tell everyone about that ghost?"

The group was silent. Thomas ignored the question and kept eating.

Marie's sister, Julie, finally spoke for the first time. She pounded her hands twice on the dining room table and then clapped them, saying "Caveman." She repeated herself three times. The rest of the family, except the Morgans chimed in. Karla added some foot stomps to the beat.

Thomas held up his hands and urged everyone to stop.

"Okay, okay, I'll share the story. I came home late from a long day at work. I looked in the mirror and noticed a stressed-out guy with circles under his eyes. I thought to myself, *buddy you're looking awful. You need to slow down. Maybe you need to listen to your wife and move to Iowa.*"

"Stop fooling around, dad," Michael said. "Tell them the truth."

"There was an alien space ship that landed. A naked caveman got out and walked up to other side of the mirror. He said, 'you look like you could use a Bud Light.'"

"That's enough, Thomas," Marie said. "Just because you thought we were making up stories about the house being haunted you think you can play games with my family about your caveman. I'm telling the story. You be quiet."

Marie cleared her throat and got a serious look on her face. "My husband has been seeing a caveman in our bathroom mirror. He described him perfectly to me. It gives me nightmares because I can see him so clearly in my mind. The caveman looks like Thomas but more crazed in the eyes. This guy even has Thomas's blue eyes. It's spooky. The first time Thomas saw him, the guy wasn't wearing any clothes. He must have escaped from a prison because his hands and feet had shackles with broken chains. The last time Thomas saw him, he was wearing some kind of white robe. His hair was clean shaven and he appeared well-rested."

"Is this from the house being haunted?" Karla interrupted.

"Could be," Marie answered. "It could also be some kind of ESP thing. Thomas comes from a family where people see things others can't see. They have visions. This has been going on for generations."

"Sounds like you guys were living in the Twilight Zone out in California," Marie's brother, Nathan, chimed in. "Why do you think the caveman was in your mirror?"

"Marie's right about one thing, the caveman does look like he could be related to me. I've been working on an ancestor project in my free time. One of my cousins is sending me some old photos and movie clips from our past. I'm wondering if someone from the 'other side' is trying to get in touch with me."

"The town still talks about how much time you spent at all the cemeteries the last time you were here, Thomas," Karla said.

"That's what inspired me to search for my family roots," Thomas said. "I traced your family history all the way back to Ireland. It's amazing how they put the hometowns on those old gravestones out here. I want to do the same thing for my side of the family."

"Just know that some people around here think you're a little peculiar wanting to hang out at the cemeteries," Nathan said. "They're already calling you guys 'those California people.'"

"I'm just getting started," Thomas said. "I found out my family came through Minnesota and Canada. When I get more information from my cousin, I'm going to dig deeper. I want to find out who this caveman is and why he's reaching out to me."

"Do you think the caveman will be visiting us here in Iowa?" Karla asked.

"I don't know," Thomas responded. "I haven't seen him since we left California."

"And we haven't heard from the other ghosts either," Michael said.

***

Karla cleared the table and brought out a fresh baked apple pie for desert. The Morgans chatted with Marie's relatives about their future plans and then headed off to bed for the evening.

Chapter Twenty-three

"Wake up, Thomas," Marie said. "You're in charge today. I'm headed off to my job interview. Make sure Michael turns in his school assignments."

Thomas couldn't believe one week passed since he arrived. He pulled the covers down and looked around at the guest room before closing his eyes again. He was weary from waking up in the middle of the night every time he heard the horns blowing from the trains passing through town. Marie kept a fan on her nightstand and it helped her to sleep but Thomas could hear the trains from miles away. He wrapped his head in a pillow to muffle the sounds but it didn't help. Marie walked over to the window and opened the blinds. The sunlight revealed Thomas' unshaven face and a head of overgrown salt and pepper hair loaded with cowlicks. The circles under his eyes were deep and dark.

Marie poked her husband several times. "Honey, there is no way you're going to get a job looking like this. You look horrible. I'm going to buy you some sleeping pills on my way home. I know you're tired. You need to get out of bed and help your son. He needs to finish his online schoolwork so we can transfer him to his new high school."

Thomas squinted his eyes and sat up. "What day is it?" He asked.

"Monday. We have five weeks to go before our friends come back. And we can't get our own place until both of us have jobs. Please stop by the barber today and get cleaned up. I love you."

Marie kissed Thomas and walked out of the bedroom. Thomas noticed how elegant she appeared in her business suit with her blonde hair pulled back and her new red eyeglasses adding some IQ points. Her calf muscles were well-defined from all the hours she spent at the gym. Marie stopped at the door and turned around. Thomas couldn't help noticing how stunning her blue eyes were that peered at him.

"What's that grin on your face, Thomas?"

"Just looking at the most beautiful woman in Iowa."

"You're delirious." Marie blew a kiss and departed.

Thomas got up and headed to the bathroom. He looked at himself in the mirror and started talking to himself. "Mirror, mirror on the wall, who's the ugliest one of all?" His reflection was so horrible that it made him laugh, revealing a tooth-paste commercial smile on his dark-complected face. His years on the tennis courts contributed a few extra lines, yet he still looked younger than his age. He leaned in the mirror and looked from side to side. "This is great," he said out loud. "Looks like my caveman buddy stayed in California."

Michael knocked on the bathroom door. "Dad, can you come help me? I'm stuck on a math problem."

"I'll be out in a minute." Thomas rinsed his face and joined his son at the kitchen table. "Have you checked in with your on-line teacher?"

"There is a two hour time difference. I'm working on my assignments independently. If you help me, I think I can get everything done in the next couple of days. I need to pass all my classes so I can be eligible for the wrestling team."

Thomas looked at his son. He had the same ice-blue eyes as Marie and he inherited Thomas' smile. He stood at nearly 6' tall and his physique was well defined from his time on the football fields and in the gym in California. Thomas asked, "how do you feel about joining the wrestling team?"

"This is my dream, dad. I've heard a lot about how serious this sport is here and I think this is going to be a great challenge for me. Once we decide which town we're going to live in, I want to meet the wrestling coach and get started. These math problems are giving me trouble. Can you help me out?"

"We all have our own problems, son. For you, it's math. For me, it's all about finding a job and finding a home for us to live. I also want to know where that caveman comes from. I haven't seen him since we left California but I can't stop thinking about him. Right now, the only thing we're going to focus on is math. Let's get to work."

Chapter Twenty-four

The doorbell rang. Roxy was the first to respond. She darted for the front door like a miniature gazelle, leaping over the Morgans belongings that were packed in cardboard boxes the living room. When she reached the front door at full speed, she slid across the linoleum in the entry way and narrowly missed slamming into it. Michael picked her up and peeked through the peep hole.

"Mama's home, Roxy. Settle down," Michael said while stroking her. Roxy had a streak of hair that stood up straight every time she heard the doorbell ring. She kept barking until she knew it was Marie. Michael opened the door and let his mother in. She kissed him and pet Roxy. "Where's your father?" she asked.

"He's in the bedroom using the internet. He's been there all day," Michael answered.

"Go get him. We're going to have a family meeting."

Michael walked back to the guest bedroom and opened the door. Thomas was on his cell phone. He put his hand up to keep Michael from speaking. Michael listened while his dad spoke.

"I don't want to waste your time looking at your place if you can't do seller financing. My realtor in California told me I'm not eligible for traditional financing due to my short sale. Have a good day." Thomas ended the call and looked at his son.

"Mom's home. She wants a family meeting," Michael said.

"I'll be right there, son," Thomas said. Thomas gathered his notes and shut down the computer. The two walked into the dining room. Marie was already sitting down.

***

"Welcome home, honey," Thomas said. "How was your job interview?" Thomas kissed her and sat down next to her.

"It went really well," Marie responded. "They want to check my references and I should be hearing back in two or three days. I feel really good about it. What about you, Thomas? Were you productive today?"

"Yes, honey. Michael turned in all his school work today. He only needed help with his math class. I made about fifty phone calls from Craig's List while he was studying. I found three people who are willing to do seller financing. All three homes are within ten miles of your siblings."

"Don't you think we should rent for a couple of years first?" Marie asked.

"I called a bunch of apartment places. Most of them don't take pets. It's better if we can buy something. You won't believe what you can get in the hundred grand range."

"Don't get me started, Thomas. I told you that four years ago but you didn't listen. And don't forget what Amber said about waiting three years before we buy again."

Michael was eager to speak. "Mom, I saw the pictures. One of the homes look like a castle. When can we go check them out?"

***

"How about when your dad and I both have jobs?" Marie turned to her husband. "Honey, I really appreciate all the work you're doing to find us a place. I'm not sure you should be spending so much time looking for a house right now. I'd feel a whole lot better if you were looking for work."

Thomas reached out and held hands with Marie. "We've only got one car right now, honey. I really can't do anything until we get our second car from California. The first thing my new boss is going to say to me is, 'when can you start?' It will look stupid if I say, 'let me check the bus schedule.'"

"We're walking a tight rope, honey," Marie said.

"With no safety net beneath us," Thomas added.

"When can we get our other car?" Michael asked.

"We have to wait until Mom gets a job. I can buy a one-way plane ticket to California when she gets her first paycheck. Once I get back, I can find a job. The unemployment rate here is less than 5%. I don't think either of us are going to be unemployed for long. That's why I'm working so hard finding us a place to move into."

"This whole process is a little scary," Marie said.

"Let's pray," Thomas said. "Bow your heads." Thomas paused for a few moments.

* * *

"Gracious and loving Father, we are thankful that you are here with us in our time of need. Thank you for leading Marie to her interview today. If it's your will, we ask that she gets a quick response and that her job offer is enough for us to meet our financial needs. Please guide Michael as he completes his requirements for the semester and help him adjust to his new school in Iowa. Please guide me to the right job and the right home for our family. Help us with our finances so that we have enough funds to pay all our bills. Amen."

Marie and Michael opened their eyes and said, "Amen."

"Why are you crying, Mom?" Michael asked.

"I can't believe I'm finally home," she said.

"This is all by God's grace," Thomas said as he passed her a tissue. "It's God's grace."

Chapter Twenty-five

"Thomas, you got a care package from your cousin," Marie said. I picked it up from the post office on my way home from my second interview.

Thomas was like a kid at Christmas. He ripped open the package and read the note inside.

***

Dear Thomas,

This project has been a labor of love these past twelve months. I hope you enjoy all the letters, poems, pictures and videos. Everything is marked so you will be able to identify all the people.

Love,

your cousin, Martha

"Look at this, Marie," Thomas said. "This is a treasure chest."

Thomas and Marie flipped through stacks of photographs.

"The family resemblance is amazing," Marie said. "You all look so much alike. Your great-grandfather looks just like your brother, Ted."

"Wow. They even have the same body posture," Thomas said.

Thomas found a genealogy chart at the bottom of the care package and opened it up. "This is exactly what I was looking for," Thomas said. "Can you believe how far back this goes?"

Marie paused for a moment and then looked directly into her husband's eyes. "Thomas, I'm nervous."

***

"What's wrong, honey?"

"We have so much work to do. I'm afraid you're going to go all OCD on me and lose yourself in this treasure chest. I need you to focus on what's important to your family -- the one that's here. Not the one in all those old photographs. Please, promise me you will put this away until we get settled."

"I'm sorry, Marie. You're right. You know how I get."

Marie raised her eyebrows.

"Well, aren't you going to ask me about my second interview?" she asked.

Thomas put everything back in the box and closed it. "Tell me everything," he said.

"There's not much to tell," Marie said, trying to hide her smile. "They called my manager in San Diego before the second interview and I got a glowing review. The only question they had was, 'when can you start?'"

Thomas wrapped his arms around his wife. "You are amazing," he said.

"We're just getting started. How soon can you go back to California to get our other car?" Marie asked.

"I already booked a flight. My tennis buddy, Clyde, offered to cash in his frequent flyer miles for a free one-way ticket so I can join him for his annual guy party. I leave next Friday morning. Clyde will pick me up at the airport. After the party I plan to pick up our car and head back home. I'll be back the following Friday."

"What about gas money for the trip home?" Marie asked.

"Since I don't need to buy a plane ticket, I'm using that money for gas. I can survive on peanut butter and jelly sandwiches while I'm driving back home."

The doorbell rang. Marie walked over to answer it while Thomas put away his care package.

Marie looked through the peep hole and opened the front door.

"Hi, mom," Michael said. Roxy was panting from the long walk. Her tongue was stretched out to its limit. Marie knelt down to greet her.

"She looks tired. Is she okay?" Marie asked.

"I took her leash off when we got to the corn fields. She ran for about a mile at full speed. I think she's out of gas now," Michael said. Roxy walked over to her water bowl and began drinking.

"Did you get the job?" Michael asked.

"I start Monday," Marie said. "And your dad leaves

Friday to get our other car. He's going to be gone a week. That means you will be home alone. Will you be able to get your online schoolwork done so we can transfer all your credits to your new high school?"

"No problem," Michael answered.

"Let's sit down together and go over our plans," Marie said.

The Morgans sat down at the dining room table and discussed their ideas for the future.

Michael asked, "What town are we going to live in?"

"It looks like the best place to live is somewhere close to where your mom grew up," Thomas said. "We need to find a place where pets are okay and the rents aren't too high. Now that your mom has a job, our chances of getting a place quickly go up big time."

"Your dad thinks we should buy a place," Marie said. "I think he's dreaming."

"Marie, give me a break. I really believe we have a shot at seller financing. I just need a couple of days to sort through all the Craig's List ads and find the right seller. A bunch more properties showed up today."

"Okay, Thomas, that's your project. If you can find us something before you leave for California, I will feel much better. We need to get Michael enrolled in high school as soon as we know what school district we'll be living in.

* * *

The timer on the stove buzzed. "What's cooking?" Marie asked.

"Stuffed pasta shells and asparagus. I had a good feeling when you left this morning that you were going be hired. This is our celebration meal," Thomas said. "Would you like a glass of wine?"

Marie nodded yes.

"I baked an apple pie for dessert," Thomas said.

"I didn't know you could bake," Marie said.

"Yep. I found the recipe online and walked over to the grocery store to get the ingredients while you were gone."

Marie appeared shocked. "Well, this sure is a nice surprise."

"I saved the best for last," Thomas said. "You aren't the only one who has news about a job."

"When are you going to share your news?" Marie asked.

"Let's enjoy our supper first. When dessert is served I'll spill the beans."

"Supper?" Michael asked.

* * *

"We don't do dinner anymore," Thomas told his son. "We're in Iowa now. Iowans eat supper in the evening and dinner around lunch time."

"You're a quick learner, honey," Marie said. "I think you're going to blend right in. And I can't wait to hear about your new job."

Marie raised her wine glass. "Let's toast to our new lives." Thomas raised his wine glass and Michael raised his glass of milk. "Cheers," they said in unison.

Chapter Twenty-six

"Please turn off all electronic equipment, buckle your seat belts and place your trays in the upright position. We are preparing for take-off," the flight attendant said.

The last passenger to board looked at Thomas. "Is that middle seat taken?" he asked.

* * *

"I'll move over and you can have the aisle seat," Thomas replied. The flight attendant stopped by and helped the passenger with his carry-on. "I'm sorry, sir, the overhead bins are full. I'll take this with me and you can claim it when we land."

"I'm Alan. How are you doing today?"

"Hi, Alan. I'm Thomas. I'm fine, thanks. And you?"

"Great. This is my first trip to San Diego. I can't wait. This trip has been hectic so far. My early morning flight out of Minnesota was delayed due to the heavy fog and I barely made this flight on time."

"I have some ancestors from Minnesota," Thomas said. "One of them was the first speaker of the House when Minnesota became a state."

"What's his name?"

"Starkey. James Starkey. I just found out about him about a week ago. One of my cousins sent me a care package with a bunch of names. This Starkey relative spent a lot of time chasing Indians when he was in the military. He got kicked out for recruiting underage kids to fight the Indians."

"Do you know what tribe?"

"Chippewa."

* * *

"That's a slang term for Ojibwe. I'm a descendent. We don't like the name Chippewa." Alan crossed his arms and tensed his body. His smile disappeared from his wrinkled face.

"Sorry. I was reading one of Starkey's stories and that's the name he used. On behalf of my family, I apologize for the Ojibwe he killed."

"Why are you going to San Diego?" Thomas asked.

"A wedding. One of my closest friends has a daughter who lives there and she's getting married tomorrow. How about you?"

"This is my first trip back since I moved away over a month ago. I'm picking up a family vehicle I left behind when I rented a moving truck."

"How long are you staying?"

"I'll be back on the road early Monday morning."

Thomas paused for a moment and started shaking his head. He looked bewildered.

"What's wrong?" Alan asked.

"I can't believe I'm talking with a real live member from the same tribe my great-great-great-great grandfather fought with."

* * *

"I'm only a quarter Ojibwe," Alan said. "My Indian blood comes from my mother's side of the family. I'm not sure about where the other side came from. All I know is there's enough Ojibwe in me to send my children to college. For me, that's a fair enough trade for my kids even though my ancestors gave the farm away. What a raw deal that was."

"What kind of work do you do, Alan?"

"I'm a dairy farmer. I've lived in Minnesota all my life. I own fifty acres of land in Northern Minnesota. It's some of the most beautiful country you will ever see, especially in the Autumn."

"I can't wait to see the leaves change color," Thomas said.

Alan looked directly into Thomas's eyes. "You are facing great change in your life. Yes, the leaves will change color. Then, it will get cold and the snow will come. Something tells me you are on a great journey. Our paths were meant to cross."

"What do you mean?" Thomas asked.

"Our grandfathers were enemies. We are friends. You have a destiny. Your ancestors are reaching out to you. They have something to say to you."

"How do you know this?"

***

"My Indian blood helps me see things others can't see. There are no coincidences. My first plane was delayed for a reason. I was supposed to be sitting here with you today to help you on your journey. Not the journey to San Diego. The bigger journey — to find your roots."

"This is crazy," Thomas said. "How can you know all this? We just met."

"My people know things. This is our gift."

"I hesitate to share with you because you will think I'm crazy," Thomas said.

"Go ahead," Alan said.

"When I lived in San Diego, we were out in the country. We lived on top of a mountain. My wife and son told me they heard things. Like ghost. Our home was built on an ancient Indian burial ground. I think the spirits were trying to reach them."

"Did you ever see or hear them?" Alan asked.

"Not until we were selling our home. One day I looked in the mirror and about had a heart attack."

"What happened?"

"I saw a crazy man. He was naked. He was staring at me."

* * *

"What did you see in his surroundings?"

"Not much. The plants were small and appeared dried up, like something you see in a desert area. There weren't any homes or buildings. The man looked like he had been in a fight and he was the loser."

"This man is also one of your great-grandfathers. He is calling you. You will go on a great journey and you will find out why he searching for you."

"I'm already on the journey of a life-time. I just moved my family over 1,800 miles."

"This is only the beginning. You have many more miles to go. You are stubborn. You never wanted to leave your home in California. It never belonged to you. The land did not belong to you. This caveman, he did not appear until you were ready to leave. Now, he is calling you. Your road map is in your heritage. The generations before you will help you to find this caveman in the mirror."

"Ladies and gentleman, the captain has turned on the seat belt sign. Please return to your seats and buckle your seat belts."

Thomas was surprised how quickly the time passed. He had so many questions. Alan closed his eyes and grasped both seat rests. Thomas turned to look out the window. The woman occupying the window seat was still sleeping.

She never spoke a word during the entire flight. Thomas spotted familiar downtown buildings and took a deep breath when he noticed the sunlight bouncing off the ocean in the horizon. The wheels hit the ground and the woman next to him jolted. She opened her eyes for the first time. Alan appeared to be meditating.

"Did you have a nice flight?" the woman seated at the window asked.

"It went really fast," Thomas responded.

"Not as fast as the rest of your journey," Alan said. "And one more thing. Don't drink too much. It's better to drink milk instead. Drinking milk is good for business."

Alan's words confirmed he was some kind of visionary. Thomas never told him about the drinking party his buddies planned for the following night. He didn't have to. Alan knew.

The plane rolled to a stop and the doors opened. Alan extended his hand to Thomas.

"Safe journey, my friend. Our paths will cross again."

The two shook hands and Alan walked away while Thomas waited for the line to clear so he could retrieve his carry-on bag. He turned on his cell phone and read the text message from Clyde.

Text me when you're out front. I'll pick you up outside the main entrance at terminal 1.

Chapter Twenty-seven

Clyde pulled up in his 1969 blue and white VW van and flashed a bright smile at Thomas.

"Good to see you, buddy. Hop in."

The van was an extension of Clyde, an avid surfer who

loved nostalgia. He knew how to have fun and the drinking games he invented were well-known on college campuses throughout the country.

"It's great to see you, Clyde. Thanks for the plane ticket and for picking me up."

"We have a full agenda, Thomas. I made a shopping list. Take a look and see if anything's missing."

Thomas looked at the list. "How many people are coming? It looks like there's enough alcohol for an army."

"Twelve including you, Thomas. I designed some of my best games ever. Think of it as a decathlon. There are preliminary rounds to get everybody in the mood. Then the real fun begins. This is competition at the highest levels."

Thomas thought about the Indian he met on the plane ride. He remembered the warning about no drinking. There was no turning back now. Clyde was so enthusiastic about the party that he could barely sit still.

"I noticed the for sale sign on your van," Thomas said. "What's up?"

"This is my dream vehicle," Clyde answered. "But it's not practical. There aren't any seat belts for my kids and it doesn't climb the mountains very well. Work is really busy and I don't get to surf much anymore. It's time to move on. Everywhere I go I get attention. People love this van."

"You don't need a van to get attention, Clyde. You have a way of attracting people into your life. Remember when I picked you up from the football game? You were wearing that crazy suit you had custom-made."

"I have a whole closet full of custom suits. When I get an idea, I call my tailor and ask him to design it for me. I even made a suit for this weekend. You can think of me as a game show host. This suit is the bomb."

Clyde turned into the grocery store parking lot and found a spot near the front door. As soon as he parked, strangers walked up to him and started talking about the van.

“Will you negotiate on the price? I want to buy your van," One of the onlookers asked.

"15,000 firm," Clyde replied. "Take my number down and call me if you're serious. Sorry, I can't talk right now, I'm on a deadline. I have to run. Let's go, Thomas."

Clyde left the crowd behind and marched into the grocery store. "We're gonna need two carts," he said. Thomas could barely keep up with him. They headed for the liquor department and filled both carts to the brim. Clyde looked at his watch. "We're going to have to hurry. There's lots to do to get ready. We'll stop for a quick dinner on the way back to my place."

***

"Someone's having a party," the check-out clerk told Clyde as he loaded up the belts.

"I wish I could invite you," Clyde said, "but this is guys only this weekend."

The clerk scribbled her name down on a notepad and offered it to Clyde. "When you open your party up to girls, make sure and call me," she said.

Thomas shook his head. "You're a babe magnet," he said.

"I'm a married man. Those days are behind me. Well, except for the games. Thomas, I can't wait for you to see what I've been building."

Clyde was one of those rare people you only meet once in a life-time. He was happy-go-lucky and lived every day to the fullest. He used his engineering background to construct drinking games using magnets and gadgets to control the flow of water. His contraptions were technological wonders.

Clyde stuck the note in his pocket and waved good-bye to the clerk. He marched back to the van where the crowd was still gathered.

"When can we talk about your van?" a middle-aged man asked.

"Tuesday." I've got a full schedule right now.

* * *

Clyde and Thomas unloaded the party supplies and climbed inside.

"I'd sure like to have a full schedule like that," the buyer said.

Clyde waved to the crowd and backed out. "Let the fun begin, Thomas. You are going to have the best weekend ever."

Chapter Twenty-eight

Clyde spotted a gas station at the corner and pulled in.

"$4.89 a gallon. Is that right?" Thomas asked.

"Some places in Southern California are over five dollars a gallon right now," Clyde responded. "Don't sweat it, I got this covered. You're not allowed to pay for anything on this trip. You're my guest."

Clyde hopped out of the van and inserted his credit card at the gas pump. While he was pumping his gas, another customer walked up to him and inquired about the for sale sign. Clyde walked over to the paper towel dispenser and pulled on it. He asked the man for a pen and jotted down his phone number on the paper towel.

"The price is firm," Clyde said. "If you're serious, call me Tuesday morning and we'll talk. I gotta run. I'm late." Clyde put the gas cap back on, got his receipt and got back inside. The other customer snapped a couple of photos of the Clyde's prized possession before Clyde drove off. He turned on the radio. Journey was singing **Don't Stop Believing**.

"I love this song," Thomas said. Clyde cranked up the music.

"Some will win and some will lose," the lead singer sang.

"That's how it's going to be this weekend, Thomas. Some will win and some will lose."

"I have faith," Thomas said.

"Thomas, I didn't buy you a plane ticket to hear you talk about your faith all weekend. I told you when I first met you I'm going to get you over to the dark side. Just wait. Scientists are about to announce they discovered the God particle. God is shrinking and science is solving all the great mysteries."

"Sorry, Clyde. You're not going to be able to get me over to the dark side. That's just not going to happen. I noticed that cross hanging from your rear view mirror. Is there something you want to tell me?"

"Ariel asked us to put it up."

"Let me get this straight. You're on the dark side but you allow Jesus to hang from your rear view mirror?"

"Our daughter is asking a lot of questions about God and I don't want to burst her bubble. It's just like Santa Claus and the Easter Bunny. She'll grow out of it."

"Is that what happened to you, Clyde, you grew out of it?"

I always asked questions. Science has most of the answers. The more advanced we get, the more answers we find. There is no God.

"You're going to break her heart, Clyde."

"What do you mean?"

"In a lot of ways she's just like you. She's asking questions. She wants to know about God. Some day you're going to have to tell her you don't believe. What's she gonna do when she finds out?"

* * *

"Thomas, do really believe that a god can exclude people from Heaven, that is, if there really is a god and there really is a Heaven?"

"God doesn't exclude people, Clyde. That's why Jesus is hanging from your rear view mirror. His Son died so everyone can have a shot at Heaven. The door's open. The only way you're excluded is if you decline the invitation."

"What invitation?"

"God is using your daughter to reach you."

"You're dreaming," Clyde said.

"Oh really? If that's true, why did Ariel ask you to put a Cross in your car? What I mean by that is everyone knows the Easter Bunny is cute and Santa is cool because he bring toys. But what about a dead man hanging from a tree? What kid in their right mind asks their daddy to put a dead man hanging from a cross inside her parents' vehicle?"

"You have a good point, Thomas. My daughter claims she's seeing things. My wife and I never once said a word about God to her. She approached us and told us she wanted us to take her to God's house."

"Do you take her?"

* * *

"Leah takes her."

"What do you do while they're in church?" Thomas asked.

"I've got enough projects around my place to last ten years. When they're at church I get a lot done."

"Tell me more about her visions," Thomas said.

"Why? They're just figments of her wild imagination. Lots of kids go through this. Ariel claims she's seeing a guy wearing a white robe."

"Because I'm seeing things, too. And I stopped being a kid a long time ago. Do you know how many years I've had this gray hair?"

"Ever since I've known you, Thomas. So, are you drinking when you see things? That happens to me all the time."

"No. I'm wide awake. No alcohol," Thomas replied.

"Ghosts?"

"No. I'm seeing a guy in a white robe."

"Jesus?" Clyde asked.

"No. But I think the guy I keep seeing is from another time. The first time I saw him he was naked. He looked crazy. He had those eyes that scare you so much you get nightmares."

"Where do you see him?"

"In the mirror."

"Does he talk to you?"

"No. He just stares."

"Sounds creepy. What does Marie think about your visions?"

"She thinks I need a vacation. She's afraid I'm cracking under all the pressure from our short sale."

"How did it go?"

"We got a buyer just in time. The clock was running and we were past the two-minute warning."

"So, what's next?"

"Just like the song says, 'don't stop believing.'"

"What about the man you see in the mirror?"

"I'm not sure. There's so much going on right now. I feel like a fish out of water. It sure was nice to see the Pacific Ocean when our plane was landing."

"Thomas, what you need right now is to enjoy your

trip. Part of the reason I wanted you to have my frequent flyer miles is so that we can have some quality time together. I don't think you'll ever convince me about your God, however, it's fun trying to figure out how your warped mind works."

"Clyde, I can't wait to see how you handle Ariel when she reaches the teenage years. Look at you. You've got Jesus in your van and you're talking to me about God."

"God particles. You're putting words in my mouth."

Thomas looked out the window. "It sure is nice to be in the mountains again. We don't have those in Iowa. A few hills but that's it."

"How long before you move back?" Clyde asked.

"That's not in the cards, Clyde. A few visits now and then but that's it. I'm being called to another life. This is only the beginning."

Chapter Twenty-nine

"This is only the beginning of what?" Clyde asked.

"Are you sure you want to talk about this now, Clyde?"

"Yes. If you're not moving back here, then what's in your cards?"

* * *

"It's like a treasure hunt. That weird guy staring at me from the other side of the mirror is my guide. He wants me to find the treasure. I'm a detective. All I have to do is dig."

"It doesn't sound like you have much to go on, Thomas. Maybe you should just move back and hang out with us on the tennis courts. The odds of you finding some kind of treasure chest are pretty small. How do you think you're going to find this caveman?"

"I think the answer is in my past. This caveman guy is one of my distant relatives."

"That's hogwash. Why do you think that?"

"Like I said, Clyde, I feel like I'm a detective. I uncovered some clues pointing to my theory."

"Go on."

"I sat next to a man who is part Indian on my plane ride over here. The tribe he's from is Ojibwe. That's the same tribe one of my ancestors fought when the state of Minnesota was still a territory. I read about his struggles with the Indians in a story he published in the early 1800's."

"What does that have to do with the caveman?"

"The Indians have a special connection to the spirit

world. They buried their dead on the same mountain we lived on before we relocated to the Midwest. All these years my family heard ghosts in our home. I never believed them until I saw the man in the mirror. All of them are connected. I just have to figure out how and why they want to connect with me."

"This sounds far-fetched, Thomas. How do you think you're gonna solve the mystery?"

"I'm connecting a lot of dots by studying my heritage. One of my cousins sent me a package with old pictures, videos and chart showing our ancestry. It turns out there are generations of writers in my family. I'm sorting through everything to see if I can find a connection to the man in the mirror."

"So Thomas, you think these dead Indians who were buried under your house, this Indian you sat next to on the plane and your ancestors are all connected, right?"

"Yes. I do believe there's a reason I'm having these visions. And the Indians have a sixth sense. Alan looked right into my eyes and warned me not to drink this weekend when I told him about our party plans."

"This weekend is a drinking marathon, Thomas. Just wait until you see the game board. It has a moat with tiny motors that make the water flow. The bottle caps spin around and all the players have to sink them. It's so unique I'm thinking about applying for a patent."

* * *

Clyde got so excited talking about his games that he took his eye off the road for a moment as he approached a curve and swerved over to the side of the road. He hit a patch of gravel and skidded to a stop. A cloud of dust enveloped the VW van. The two man stared at each other.

"Are you okay?" a man asked who pulled in behind Clyde.

Clyde gave him a thumbs up and the man got back on the road.

"That was scary," Clyde said. He waited for the road to clear before pulling out.

"Clyde, you only mentioned drinking and you almost got us killed. Alan, the Indian I met on the plane, warned me to be cautious this weekend."

"Stop worrying, Thomas. You'll be staying at my place all weekend and everyone in the group will be off the road. My wife is visiting her sister and we have the place to ourselves. Just don't tell anyone about your visions or they'll think you lost your marbles."

"Deal," Thomas said.

"I'm interested in learning more about where my family came from," Clyde said. "How much progress have you made finding your roots?"

* * *

"Not much. I'm planning to drive to Minnesota to learn more about my great-great-great grandfather. There's great information about where people came from on the gravestones. It looks like some of my ancestors settled in Canada first when they left Ireland. One of them set up a brewery in Canada during the prohibition. He sent a case of beer to the White House in an effort to convince Roosevelt to lift the prohibition."

"How about we raise a toast to your ancestors during our drinking decathlon? I didn't know you Morgans were responsible for ending the prohibition."

"There's a lot more, Clyde. I'll be happy to share with you when I uncover the facts."

Chapter Thirty

"Where am I?" Thomas felt Chico's tongue stroking the side of his face. He opened his eyes and saw a massive tongue from Clyde's watchdog, a large white Hungarian Kuvasz. Thomas sat up and looked at the beer bottles all around him and tried to remember why he was sprawled out on the floor. The motor was still running on the battleship game Clyde set up for the party a few feet away. The water in the moat flowed over a collection of bottle caps at the bottom of the moat.

***

Clyde walked into the kitchen, opened the refrigerator door and pulled out the last remaining bottle of beer, unaware Thomas was on the dining room floor. Chico walked over to his master and wagged his tail. Thomas called out to the master of ceremonies, "What happened last night?"

"You don't remember?" Clyde asked. "We sunk your battleship all night long. Every time you lost, You drank a beer and then you challenged all of us to a rematch. At 2:00 AM we ran out of beer so we called it a night. They're all still sleeping. You were too drunk to make it to the guest room so we decided to leave you on the floor when you passed out."

"What are you doing drinking?" Thomas asked.

"It's the best way to beat a hangover. I stashed this last one in the fridge before we ran out last night. I can't believe all those cases of beer are gone." Clyde was still wearing his custom suit.

"You look like a game show host, Clyde. I'm surprised you don't have any wrinkles in your suit."

"I told my suit guy this suit needs to be heavy duty. The material is super expensive. See? You can even sleep in it and it stays wrinkle free." Clyde maneuvered through the beer bottles and bottle caps strewn all over the floor and opened the sliding glass door for his dog to go outside. The patio looked like a war zone.

***

"My wife is coming home today, Thomas. I need you and the guys to help me clean the place up." Clyde chugged the last of his beer and set the bottle down on the counter.

"You put on quite a show last night, Thomas. It was worth all those frequent flyer miles I cashed in to get you your ticket."

"I don't remember a thing," Thomas said.

"You behaved like a drunk sailor. I've never seen you cuss — not ever. Well, last night your language was so foul you even embarrassed me. And you were waving your middle finger like it was some kind of sword. It got so bad that the other guys offered to drink your beer when you lost so you wouldn't pass out. I finally had to call a time out to get some food in you. During our food break you started talking about all the ghosts in your life."

Thomas got up off the floor and sat down at the dining room table. "I told the guys about the ghosts?"

"Thomas, you spilled the beans about your old house being haunted. You even imitated how they taunted your wife and son. You looked like a zombie last night. The best part of the night was when you shared your story about the caveman you keep seeing in the mirror. Your imitation of the caveman was award-winning. And you told the guys you're going all over the world to track him down. Then you got up to use the bathroom for about the tenth time and when you came back you told everyone you found the caveman in my mirror. You were freaking all of us out."

"That's the only part of the night I remember, Clyde. I wasn't hallucinating. The caveman was in your bathroom mirror. He was signaling me to come to him. I will never forget that face."

"All I can say, Thomas, is that when you came out of the bathroom you were spooked."

"I have to find him, Clyde. He's out there somewhere."

"What you need to help me find right now is all the beer bottles and the bottle caps, Thomas. I don't want my wife to put a moratorium on our guys night."

The rest of the group entered the room behind Thomas and crept up on him. They had their arms extended and their eyes closed. "Boo," they yelled in unison. Thomas cringed.

"That's not funny," he said.

"Where are you, Thomas?" the group asked. "We're looking for you. Why did you build a house on our burial ground? And why did your ancestors kill us?"

Thomas sighed. "You guys need to swear not to tell anyone about my story. My wife will kill me if she finds out I told you about our house being haunted. And I'm not sure what the caveman will do to me if he thinks you're mocking him."

Clyde reassured Thomas. "Don't worry, Thomas, your secret is safe with us — on one condition. You need to help get this place cleaned up before my wife comes home."

"Yeah, Thomas. Clyde is right. What happens in Vegas stays in Vegas," Peter said. "Too bad I have to leave you guys but I need to get back to my family. Our son has a soccer game and I'm in charge of lining the field."

The rest of the men started cleaning the place up. Any time they got near Thomas, they pretended to be zombies just to get under Thomas's skin. Two hours later there was no evidence about what happened the night before.

Chapter Thirty-one

Thomas got out of the shower and dried himself off. He was too afraid to look in the mirror now that he was sober. The mist covering the mirror offered a temporary layer of protection but it was dissipating quickly.

"Are you almost ready?" Clyde asked, knocking on the

bathroom door. "I need to take Chico for a walk. You should come with us so you can get your blood flowing again."

"Just give me a couple more minutes and I'll join you," Thomas responded.

Thomas stared into the mirror after he put on his t-shirt and jeans. He noticed the bags under his eyes. The long nap he took after helping the men clean up didn't do much to help him with his hangover or his disheveled appearance.

Alan was right, he thought. *Drinking is bad.* The Indian he met on the plane knew this weekend was going to be rough but Thomas was too stubborn to drop out in the middle of the challenge. Thomas opened the door and walked back into the kitchen where Clyde and his pet were waiting.

"Take these," Clyde said, handing him a couple of aspirin and a glass of water. "You need all the help you can get to recover from your hangover. Let's go for a walk."

Thomas swallowed his aspirin and headed out the door with Clyde and Chico. "We walk two miles every day, Thomas. Do you think you can handle that in your condition?"

"As long as you don't ask me too many questions," Thomas replied. "My head hurts."

* * *

"I talked with Leah and she thinks you should stay in the guest room one more night before you get back on the road. What do you think?"

"That would be great, Clyde."

"Just make sure you don't talk about three things when my family gets home. Don't talk about our drinking games in front of Ariel. And whatever you do, please don't bring up anything about your ghosts, your caveman or Jesus. You really rattled me when you were going on your rant during your drunken stupor."

"Don't blame me, Clyde. You're the one who concocted all those drinking games."

"True. But you crossed the line. I was trying you save you from going too far but you kept taunting all the guys. Every one of them is a type A. They hate to lose. And every time you challenged them, they ganged up on you. I tried changing the rules but you wouldn't let me help you. You were a madman."

"I was trying to get the caveman out of my head," Thomas said. "I'm not seeing ghosts. This guy is real. I have to find him."

"How are you going to do that?" Clyde asked.

"There are some pretty good clues in my family tree. That Indian I met on the plane ride over here gave me a great idea. He told me my road map was tied to my ancestors. I dreamed about what's ahead while I was passed out on your floor during the party. And I know who is going to help me."

"Who?"

"Wendy."

"Who's Wendy?"

"She reached out to me on the internet. She's from a lost branch of my family."

"How did you find her?"

"She found me. I posted some inquiries about distant relatives and she contacted me. It turns out we are related through my father's side of the family. When she turned 18 she found out she was adopted."

"So, you're blood related?" Clyde asked.

"Yes. And she is part Indian from the other side of her family."

"Ojibwe?"

"No. Another tribe."

"So, what's the deal with all these Indians that are popping into your life all of a sudden?" Clyde asked.

* * *

"I don't know. The Indian I met on the plane told me the caveman waited to show up until I was ready for my journey. When I find the caveman, I believe I will find the answers."

"I still don't know how you're going to find someone who keeps showing up in the mirror, Thomas. This whole thing is getting crazy. I'm thinking maybe you're pulling some kind of prank on me. So, where are the hidden cameras?"

"I'm serious, Clyde. Yes, this whole thing is freaking me out a little bit. I just met Wendy a couple of weeks ago. She's been digging really deep into our heritage. I'm the first living relative she's contacted. We haven't even met yet. Just some phone calls and file sharing."

"Where does she live?"

"Minnesota. Her grandmother has a lot of stories about my ancestors. I talked to her for over an hour and took about ten pages of notes. She knew why the family split apart. A whole branch of my family disappeared. Now they're back. Just like Alan predicted."

"I'm not following, Thomas. How does this guy you just met on the plane ride over here know all these things about you and your ancestors?"

"Clyde, I really can't explain it. All I know is that some really weird stuff is going on. The spirit world is reaching out to me. My ancestors are calling me."

"Why, Thomas? Why? You know I don't believe in spirits. I'm from the dark side. My goal is to get you on the dark side. You know what I'm talking about. We have been having this conversation for a long time. Your ancestors are dead. There all no spirits. You're just off your rocker. When you die you turn into dust. That's what the dark side is — emptiness. Nothing. Zilch. There is no afterlife."

"I'm not stopping until I find the caveman, Clyde. Wendy told me she's willing to help me. She's been on this journey for over ten years now. I just started."

Clyde pointed to his house. "We're back," he said.

"That was fast," Thomas said.

"Yep. It was a giant loop which is just like our conversation. It's all going round and round in one big circle. When you die I'm going to ask your wife if we can cut open your brain and see what's going on in there."

"You can joke all you want, Clyde, but that's not going to stop me. The wheels are in motion and I'm going to find out who this guy is that keeps showing up in the mirror."

"Whatever you say, Thomas. Just keep your mouth shut when the rest of my family comes home. Remember — no caveman, no ghosts, no spirits and no Jesus around the dinner table tonight. Tomorrow morning we'll say goodbye; you can take your caveman and all your other spirits back to Iowa with you. Okay?"

"Deal."

Chapter Thirty-two

"Thomas, are you awake?" Clyde asked from the hallway outside the guest room.

"I am now," Thomas responded.

"It's dinner time. I just got a text from Leah. She's picking us up beer and pizza. They're on their way home now.

"I think I'll skip the beer," Thomas said. "I'll be out in a few minutes."

* * *

Thomas got out of bed, opened the door and walked over to the bathroom. When he turned the light on his eyes burned. He splashed some water on his face to wake himself up. After he dried his eyes, he took another look in the mirror. His eyes were still blood shot and the dark circles hadn't departed, even though he slept most of the day. His stomach growled at him while he stared at his disheveled reflection. Thomas wet his hands and tried to straighten his clumped-up hair.

Chico announced Leah and Ariel's return with several loud barks outside the garage door. Clyde rushed over to greet his family. "My ladies are home," he shouted. Leah was carrying two large pizzas and a paper bag with a couple of six-packs of beer. She set everything down on the dining room table and wrapped her arms around Clyde while Ariel greeted Chico. Thomas looked at the couple and covered his eyes. "You two need to get a room," he said.

"Give us a break," Clyde said. "We haven't seen each other for three days."

"You don't look so good, Thomas," Leah said. "Were you the biggest loser last night?"

"Yep, but I'm not allowed to talk about it."

"Who wants to eat?" Clyde asked.

Ariel was the first one to take a seat at the dining room

table. Leah opened up the pizza boxes while Clyde served the beer.

"You need this, Thomas," Clyde said, handing him his first beer since the party.

Ariel waited for everyone to be seated and then asked, "Mommy, is it okay if I lead the prayers tonight?" The question caught Thomas by surprise since he knew Clyde had no interest in religion. He looked at Clyde to see the expression on his face but Clyde already had his head bowed.

"Go ahead, honey," Leah responded.

"Dear Jesus, thank you for keeping us safe. Please watch over all the soldiers who are fighting for our freedom and please help Thomas get back home safely to his family. Thank you for the pizza. Amen."

"You're really good at that, Ariel. Thank you for praying for me."

"You're welcome," the six-year-old with two missing front teeth replied.

"Me and mommy take turns."

"What about your daddy?"

Clyde looked sternly at Thomas, trying to hush him up.

* * *

"Jesus told me that daddy doesn't isn't ready to talk to him yet. He said not to worry about it and just keep taking turns praying with mommy before we eat."

"Do you talk to Jesus every day, Ariel?" Thomas asked.

"Yes."

"And does He talk to you?"

"Yes."

"What does he say?"

"He told me today that He was going to help you find the man you're looking for?"

"What man?"

"He is one of Jesus' friends."

"Have you ever seen Jesus?"

"I see him every day when daddy drives me to school. He's hanging on the Cross from the mirror inside Daddy's van."

"And what about the man I'm looking for? Have you ever seen him?"

"No. But Jesus told me the man is looking for you."

* * *

"Why is he looking for me?"

"He knows who Jesus is. He knows the secret."

"What secret?"

"About who Jesus is. When you find the man, he will tell you the secret."

"Where will I find him?"

"Far away."

Clyde and Leah watched their daughter talk about Jesus and could not believe their eyes. They remained silent while Thomas and Ariel continued for several minutes. Clyde turned toward Thomas and asked, "Can you step outside on the patio with me?"

The two men opened the patio door and walked outside while Leah and Ariel finished their pizza.

"What are you doing, Thomas? I thought I asked you not to talk about Jesus around my daughter."

"Your daughter has a gift, Clyde. Don't you see that?"

"What my daughter has is an over-active imagination. She's been telling stories like that ever since she learned to talk. I think it comes from her children's books."

"So, you read her children's books about Jesus?"

* * *

"No. She started talking about Jesus all by herself. That's why Leah takes her to church."

"Clyde, she knows about my caveman."

"You're full of it, Thomas. My daughter is making up stories and she's got you believing them. I'm an atheist, remember? She will grow out of this."

"Clyde, I'm going to make you a promise. I'm going to find the caveman and I'm going to learn his secret. It's no coincidence that your daughter is talking about the caveman at the dinner table."

"Just do me a favor, Thomas. No more talk about Jesus or the caveman around my family. Okay?"

"Yes."

The two men walked back into the dining room and sat down.

"When are you going home?" Leah asked.

"Sunrise tomorrow morning."

"And when are you going to look for the man?" Ariel asked.

"I don't have any other plans to look for anyone right now, Ariel. I just want to get back home and get settled."

* * *

"Will you tell me the secret when you find him?" Ariel asked.

"How about I tell your daddy first and if he says it's okay, I will talk to you?"

"That sounds like a great idea, you big loser," Clyde said.

"I thought we weren't go to talk about our activities from last night," Thomas said.

"Yeah, right. And we weren't going to talk about Jesus or the caveman either."

"I wish I could have been here last night," Leah said.

"And I just wish I could remember last night," Thomas added.

"Well, let's just say Thomas is the biggest loser," Clyde said. "Too bad he can't stay longer. He sure knows how to entertain a crowd. I'm going to miss him when he's gone."

Chapter Thirty-three

Thanks for the memories and for the plane ticket. I'll call you when I get back to Iowa, Thomas wrote.

He placed the note on the refrigerator and headed out the front door. The morning sun was getting ready to pop up from the Cuyamaca mountains just beyond the Cleveland National Forest to the east. The neighbors were still sleeping. Thomas got inside his Honda and started up the engine. The noise from the aftermarket muffler blared like a trumpet. The next door neighbor's dog woke up and summoned all of his friends. Their barks echoed through the community. Thomas backed out of the steep driveway and drove away. When he reached the first stop sign, he called Marie from his cell phone.

"How are you doing, honey?" his wife asked.

"Much better today. My headache is all gone and I'm well rested. How are you?"

"We miss you. Michael and I have been looking at all the pictures in the care package your cousin sent you. Now I understand you better."

"What do you mean, Marie?"

"Do you remember when we were dating and I asked you if you had any desire to go into politics?"

"Yes."

"There's a photo in your care package from the House of Representatives in Minnesota. It's 140 years old. You're related to the speaker of the house."

"I know, honey. It's James Starkey. I met a guy on the plane ride over here who is a descendent of the same Indian tribe James fought before he went into politics."

"It's in your blood, my love. I'm so glad you promised me you would never go into politics."

***

"Don't worry, honey. That's not in the cards for me. Why were you looking at the care package?"

"We miss you, Thomas. Michael and I thought it would be a good idea to sort through everything and learn more about where you came from. I can't believe how much you look like your ancestors."

"Marie, I have so much to share with you. This trip has been amazing."

"Did you survive Clyde's party?"

"Barely. I don't remember much but Clyde says I came in last place in every event."

"Did you get to visit the old neighborhood?"
"No. I spent most of my free time sleeping. My hangover was terrible."

"When will you be home?"

"Three days if the weather holds up."

"That's pushing it, Thomas. Maybe you should take an extra day and slow down a little."

"I'd rather get home right away and get back to my job search, Marie."

"Well, if you get tired, promise me you'll pull over and

get some rest. We want you home in one piece."

"I promise."

"One more thing, Thomas. Michael and I have been talking about your caveman. Have you seen him since you got back to California?"

"Yes. And a few people on this trip talked to me about him, too. There's a whole bunch of weird things going on about him. It's kind of spooky."

"Well, Thomas, at least Michael and I haven't seen or heard any ghosts since we sold our home and got out of California."

"That's great news, Marie. But I'm pretty sure my caveman is not a ghost. He's real. And the other people I've talked with about him are telling me to go find him."

"How are you going to do that?"

"You and Michael can help me. Keep going through the care package. Find out as much as you can about where my ancestors came from. James Starkey is part of the mystery. Look him up on the internet. I need to know the names of the towns where my family came from."

"Why?"

"Because I think the caveman is one of my distant

relatives. He wants to share a secret with me."

"There you go again, Thomas. You're delusional."

"Marie, when I get home I'll tell you the whole story. Right now I gotta go. The roads are getting really curvy. I love you."

"Bye, honey. Be safe."

Chapter Thirty-four

Thomas reached for the packet of disks Clyde gave him and inserted the first one into his CD player. He thought about what Clyde said when he handed it over. "Make sure you listen to this on your way home. It's about a guy, Louie Zamporini, who goes through hell but remains unbroken. He's a lot like you, Thomas," Clyde told him the night before Thomas departed.

Louie's biography unfolded one chapter at a time while Thomas headed back to his new home. The narrator's voice was soft and soothing, like James Earl Jones. It helped Thomas stay awake. Each captivating chapter was filled with a new catastrophe. Most of the book dealt with Louie's adventures in a Japanese concentration camp. Thomas couldn't stop thinking why Clyde wanted him to listen to the story on the road trip home, especially because Louie became a man of faith. *Why would an atheist be inspired by this man?* he thought. Thomas had three days to listen to Zamporini's story and let it all soak in. Time seemed to stand still while Thomas sped along the highway. He climbed to 13,000 feet in the Colorado mountains and parked his car at a rest stop. The cold winds sent a chill through his bones as soon as he opened the door. Thomas pulled out the air force jacket Clyde gave him as a parting gift and put in on. He zipped it up as far as it could go and added a beanie. A blanket of snow one foot thick covered the area surrounding the rest stop. Thomas decided to go on a short hike to get some pictures.

Will I be able to remain unbroken, like Louie Zamporini? Thomas thought. *Can a California man survive weather like this when he's transplanted to Iowa? And what about the caveman? Will I ever be able to meet him?* Thomas was filled with doubt about what was ahead. He tried to look strong when he talked about his future but he wasn't sure if he had what it took to remain unbroken. At 13,000 feet he was at another pinnacle in his life. Iowa was only two states away. He had no clue how far away the caveman was or how long it would take to find him. He prayed aloud and his breath puffed out clouds of smoke.

"Gracious and loving Father, I need you. I really don't have a clue why I'm on this journey. I don't even know if

I have the resources to complete my journey. I feel like I'm running on fumes. Please send me your Spirit to guide me. Help me get off this mountain and get back to my family. Please help me to be unbroken, just like you helped Louie Zamporini overcome all his challenges. I'm ready for whatever you ask of me. Just promise me you will show me the way."

Thomas let out one more big breath and a cloud of smoke floated out of his mouth. He could see a rainbow inside the mist.

"Thank you, Jesus," he said. The cloud vaporized and the rainbow disappeared. Thomas turned back toward his Honda and hiked back to the parking lot, inspired that he was not alone and confident he would remain unbroken on his journey.

Chapter Thirty-five

"I am unbroken," Thomas repeated the words over and over as he made his gradual descent from the Colorado mountains. The snow was losing its tug-of-war at the lower elevations and finally acquiesced, revealing a full palette of colors along the highway cutting through the steep cliffs. The sun cast long shadows from the tall pines dotting both sides of the winding road.

"This is so beautiful," Thomas said out loud. "I wish my family were with me right now to see this."

Suddenly, everything went dark. Thomas turned on his

headlights as he drove through the mile-long tunnel. It was strange how quickly everything changed. During his time inside the cave, Thomas pondered his future. Thomas thought, *Is this how my life is going to be? Am I going to be living in darkness?* The flash of sunlight at the end of the tunnel blinded him for a moment. Thomas yelled, "I am unbroken." Then he entered the next tunnel. His mantra was working. The darkness lost its power over him. Thomas was not afraid.

Once he exited the last tunnel, Thomas prayed. "Dear Lord, thank you for being with me on this trip. I'm not afraid of the plans you have for me. I know there will be some dark days ahead. I don't know where I will be living and I don't know what kind of work I will be doing. The only thing I know for sure, Lord, is that you will be with me. Please, Jesus, just give me the strength to get through the dark days and give me the wisdom to understand what you want me to do with my life. Please help me to not go crazy. If this caveman I'm seeing in the mirror is real, help me to find him. Are you sending him to me, Jesus? Who is he? Why can't I get him out of my mind? Please, Jesus, help me to remain unbroken."

Thomas felt a vibration coming from his pocket. He pulled over to the side of the road and checked to see who was calling.

"How are you doing, Thomas?" his wife asked.

"I was just thinking about you, honey," he answered. "I'm coming out the mountains now in Colorado. It's so beautiful here. I want to take you back here with the rest of the family."

"Let's get jobs and a place to live first, okay Thomas?"

"Yes, my love. And when we do we will come back here for our summer vacation."

"When will you be home?"

"Tomorrow night. I can't wait to see you, Marie."

"Me too. I'm feeling really good about our future, Thomas."

"I am unbroken."

"What?"

"I am unbroken. I will tell you more about it when I see you, my love. It has to do with something my buddy gave me."

"Are you feeling okay, Thomas?"

"Better than ever, honey. We have a great future ahead of us. I need to get back on the road now. I love you."

"I love you, too, Thomas. Drive safe and I will see you tomorrow night."

Chapter Thirty-six

Thomas strained his eyes to read the sign on the side of the interstate. It was barely visible as the last remnants of daylight succumbed to evening. ***The People of Iowa Welcome You, Fields of Opportunities***. Thomas grinned. There were miles and miles of fields all around him. "This is my new land of opportunity," he shouted. He checked his rear view mirror. There was nothing behind him but an empty interstate that stretched in one long straight line all the way to the setting sun. The radio station turned to static. Thomas searched for a new station but there weren't many choices.

Carrie Underwood's voice blared out. It was one of the few country songs Thomas recognized. He remembered how animated his wife and son got when they would join in to the words from the song, **Before He Cheats**. They loved pretending to swing a baseball bat to the headlights while singing the words. His mind flashed back to one single moment in time when his wife was so angry she wanted to whack him over the head with a baseball bat. She told him how sad she felt on the inside because she was so far away from her family. But Thomas refused to listen to her. Giving in to her longings to return home to her family would mean saying goodbye to California. Thomas listened to the lyrics and remembered Marie's anger. That was the defining moment in their marriage. When he looked into her eyes, he knew it was time for change. It was time to put his wife first.

Thomas searched for a new station. Nothing else was clear except for the lone country station. Thomas wondered, *do they listen to anything else out here besides country?* It didn't matter. Thomas was all in. He thought about the welcome to Iowa sign. The sign at the border was a new beginning, like a new chapter in a book. *This chapter is going to be really special,* he thought. *I'm going to get busy and carve out a new life here.* His cell phone interrupted his daydreaming.

"Howdy, Marie, how are you doing, partner?" He asked.

"What's all this howdy stuff, Thomas? Are you turning country on me after all these years?"

"Just listening to some country music and thinking

about you."

"It must be the only station, Thomas."

"Yes it is. I'm in Iowa now and should be home in a couple of hours. Do you miss me?"

"Yes I do, honey. I can't wait to see you."

"Me too, my lady. What's new?"

"Michael and I are getting excited about our new home. Do you think you can find us one soon?"

"Marie, we've come a long way in such a short period time. Remember, the jobs come first before we get our own place. I've been doing a lot of thinking on this road trip and I'm getting excited, too."

"Alright honey. You're almost home. Be safe. We're waiting for you."

Chapter Thirty-seven

Thomas blew a kiss into the phone and said goodbye to his wife. He pushed the search button on the radio and found a Christian station with a faint signal. He listened to the lyrics of an unfamiliar song entitled Believer, by the group Audio Adrenaline. The words were scratchy at first, but the signal grew stronger. He listened intently and sang along...

I want to live this life unsafe, unsure, but not afraid
What I want is to give all I got somehow
Giving up letting go of control right now

'Cause I'm already out here, blind but I can see
I see the way You're moving

God how I believe that

(Chorus)
I can push back the mountains, can stand on the waves
I can see through the darkness, I'll hold up the flame
Take me to the ocean I wanna go deeper
I'm not afraid no, I'm a believer

And so I lose this life to find my way and come alive
They can try to deny what's inside of me
But there is more, can't ignore all the things unseen

'Cause I'm already out here, blind but I can see
I see the way You're moving
God how I believe that

Chorus

I believe I can walk on water with You, Lord

When I walk through the valley of the shadows
When I'm trapped in the middle of the battle
I will trust in You
'Cause trouble comes, but You never let it take me
I hold fast 'cause I know that You will save me
I will trust in You
I will trust in You

Thomas noticed a large buck frozen like a statue on the side of the interstate who appeared to be staring at him. He turned on his bright lights to get a better look. The chorus was singing "I can see through the darkness, I'll hold up the flame." Suddenly, a doe darted out from behind the buck and leaped out onto the interstate. Thomas swerved to his left but it was too late. The doe collided with the front right side of the car, sending the vehicle into a 360° counter-clockwise spin across the interstate. The deer was thrown onto the windshield and shattered the glass, making it impossible for Thomas to see as he spun toward a fast-moving semi that was passing Thomas on the left lane. The sound of the horn was like a freight train. Thomas's hands were in a death grip on the steering wheel. The semi swerved to the left and glanced the left side of the vehicle, shooting Thomas back to the right side of the interstate in a clockwise motion. The car skidded off the interstate and plunked head-first into a ditch. The airbag exploded and smothered Thomas. He came to an abrupt halt at the bottom of the ditch. The deer was lifeless on the shattered glass. The front of the car looked like an accordion and the driver's door was pressing against Thomas's legs.

Thomas opened his eyes and peeled his head off of the steering wheel. The final verse of the song was playing...

Oh here I stand all alone waiting on you, Lord
Waiting on You

Chorus

He looked up and saw his reflection in the cracked rear view mirror dangling from the smashed windshield. Streams of blood were flowing from both nostrils.

A young blonde woman wearing a bright yellow Iowa Hawkeyes sweatshirt and a black bandana ran down the embankment and banged on the driver's window.

"Are you okay?" she shouted.

Thomas didn't answer. He just looked at her as she tried to pry the door open. Two more men raced to the scene of the accident. They ran around to the passenger side of the vehicle and opened the door.

"We've gotta get him out of here, there's gas leaking," one of the men said. Thomas watched one of the men unbuckle his seat belt. The girl was already on the phone talking to the 911 operator.

"There's one man in the vehicle," she said. "He's trapped. His legs are pinned. Hurry. The car is leaking gas."

"Is he conscious?" the operator asked.

"Barely. He's not talking."

"I'm going to stay on the phone with you. The paramedics are about ten minutes away."

"Tell them you need the jaws of life," one of the men shouted to the young women.

"We need the jaws of life to get him out," she said.

* * *

A dozen cars parked on the side of the interstate and people were rushing in to see what was going on.

"Stay back," one of the men shouted. "We have a gas leak down here."
"What's your name?" the second man asked.

Thomas just stared back.

"There's a cell phone down there," one of the men said, looking in from the passenger side. "Can you see it?" The first man reached down and picked it up of the floor. He handed it to the blonde. "See if you can find the last person he talked to and call them," he said. The blonde searched his call list and called.

"Hi honey, are you almost home?" Marie asked.

"Hello, this is Tara. I'm on the side of Interstate 80. The man in the car is alive but he can't speak. The paramedics will be here any minute. Can you give us this man's name?"

"Oh my God, He's my husband. His name is Thomas. Thomas Morgan."

"Hold on one moment, ma'am." Tara juggled two cell phones and switched back to the 911 operator. "His name is Thomas Morgan."

"Thomas Morgan. Got it. Can you find out if he is allergic to any medications?" The operator asked Tara.

"Is your husband allergic to anything?" Tara asked Thomas's wife.

Marie was sobbing. "No," she cried.

"We're losing him," one of the men shouted.
Tara switched back to the operator. "He's losing consciousness."

"What's going on?" Marie asked.

"Don't worry, ma'am, the paramedics are pulling up now. Your husband is going to be okay."

"You can hang up now," the operator told Tara. "Thanks for your help. The paramedics will take it from here."

Tara hung up her phone and switched back to Marie. "Mrs. Morgan, I'm going to stay on the line with you and keep you informed. Please don't worry. Your husband is going to be okay."

Thomas closed his eyes and stopped breathing.

Chapter Thirty-eight

Thomas opened his eyes. His body was flat on the ground, covered in a light mist. He couldn't hear anything and he couldn't see anything except the fog encasing his body.

"Am I dead?" he asked. His voice echoed three times and disappeared.

A hand reached in through the mist and signaled Thomas to get up. Thomas grabbed the hand and rose to his feet.

* * *

"It's you. You're the man on the other side of the mirror who has been stalking me. Where am I? And who are you?"

The man standing directly in front of Thomas was clean-shaven and wore a seamless white garment with a hood. He answered in a soft voice. His accent was unfamiliar and the language he spoke was gibberish, yet Thomas understood every word.

"You are from me. I'm from long ago."

"How long ago?"

"20 times one hundred times our planet circled around the great light that warms your planet."

"2,000 years?"

"Yes."

"And we are related?"

"Yes."

"Are we both dead?"

"We are apart from our bodies. We're not dead. See?"

The stranger poked Thomas in the chest.

* * *

"That hurt," Thomas cried.

"If you were dead, you could not feel."

"Where's my body?"

"It's not time to show you, my son from many sons. Right now the others are working on it."

"So, am I going to die?"

"Some day, but not today. You have work to do. I've been waiting for you for a long time."

"Why do you look so young?"

"We always look better in our spirit bodies."

"Like ghosts?"

"Yes, like ghosts. Your wife and son have been trying to tell you about the spirits but your mind is thick. It took all of my life energy to reach you from the other side of your reflection."

"Why are the ghosts pestering my family?"

"You disturbed their bones when you built your home on the sacred mountain."

"The home was already there when we moved in. I don't understand."

***

"When you added rooms to your home, your tractors touched the bones of the earth people who were sleeping in their graves."

"The Indians?"

"Yes. The brothers of the Minnesota earth people who one of my sons and one of your fathers killed in the time of expansion. They are from the Ojibwe."

"I know about this man. You are talking about Captain James Starkey. I read about him when I was studying about my genealogy."

"Yes. He is a fighter, just like many in the generations that separate us. I've been watching them from the other side of their reflections, always waiting for what is to become."

"What is to become?" Thomas asked.

"I can't tell you, my son. I can only give you the signs."

"How do you know what is to become and why can't you tell me?"

"I know because I was once one with the people from the other side. They are the fallen ones."

"Devils?"

***

"Yes. They lived inside of me for many moons."

"What's your name?" Thomas asked.

"Bedrock. I am the invisible one."

"But I can see you."
"Only because you've been picked."

"Picked for what?"

"To lead the lost back home to the Father. You will do this during the trials."

"Why me?"

"Why *not* you, my son? This is in your blood. It's from me. This was passed down to you from the kings who once ruled Ireland. It's from Captain James Starkey. It's from every ancestor who came before you."

"I don't understand."

"You inherited a gift, the gift of knowing how to stop the people from the other side, the ones who once lived in my body."

"I don't have a clue what you're talking about."

"I will give you one clue to think about. Then you will go back to your body. We will meet again and I will help you to prepare."

* * *

"What's happening? Where is the light going?"

"The others are calling you back. When you wake up, remember the clue. It's part of what is to become."

"I can't see you. Hurry. Tell me the clue. I'm losing you."

"Remember the bees, Thomas. They're going to disappear from the planet. That's the first sign. Good-bye, my son. Go to sleep now. You need the rest."

Chapter Thirty-nine

"Where are the bees?" Thomas mumbled.

"Call the doctor. He's waking up," Marie shouted.

"Mom, push the button. It's right next to you," Michael said.

Moments later, the doctor rushed in and reached for the hospital chart before approaching Thomas.

"Thomas, can you hear me?" Dr. Ricketts asked.

"Yes, but I can't see you. Where am I?"

* * *

"You're at Mercy Hospital. Your wife and son are with you. Do you remember what happened to you?"

"I hit a dear while driving home from California."

"It was a close call, Thomas. We almost lost you several times. You've been sleeping for three days."

"Why can't I see you, doctor."

"It's the bandages. You have some head wounds."

"That explains the nightmares."

"Don't worry, Thomas, you're going to be fine. You need to rest."

Marie reached out and stroked Thomas on his forehead. "We've been by your side the whole time you've been sleeping, honey. Michael and I are here. How are you feeling?"

"I'm so tired, honey. I wish I could see you right now."

"You really scared us, dad. The doctors weren't sure if you were going to make it," Michael said.

Dr. Ricketts added some comments to the chart and turned to Marie and Michael. "You need to let him rest. You can stay in the room but he needs to sleep."

"Are the bees okay?" Thomas asked.

* * *

"I think he's delirious, doctor," Marie said.

"Don't worry about the bees, Thomas," Dr. Ricketts said. "They're all fine. Now go to sleep."

Everyone in the hospital room quit talking. Thomas listened to the steady beat of the machines his body was hooked up to. "The bees are fine. Nothing to worry about. I'm just hallucinating," he mumbled as he drifted back to sleep.

"No Thomas, they're not fine. The bees are dying." Bedrock scolded.

"I can't see you," Thomas said.

"Stand up," Bedrock ordered.

As soon as Thomas stood up, the fog faded and he saw Bedrock in front of him.

"What's going on?" Thomas asked.

"We don't have much time," Bedrock said. "I need to give you the other clues."

"The doctor and my wife said the bees are fine."

"They don't know yet, Thomas. Soon, they will all know. Pay attention. This is very important."

* * *

"I'm ready."

"Your government already knows what's wrong. They have the power to listen to every conversation in the world. The only place they can't reach is here. This is the in-between. They cannot come here. They don't know about the return."

"What is the return?"

"The return will happen after the war?"

"What war?"

"World War III. It starts because there is not enough food."

"That doesn't make sense. There is plenty of food."

"Not after the bees die."

"You never told me why the bees die."

"The place where you live now is at the center of the problem. They changed the seeds. They went too far. These seeds are all over the world. And the bees cannot pollinate. No bees means no corn. That's when the fighting begins. There won't be enough food. They already know this in Russia. That's why the man in charge is invading his neighbors. The world thinks it's because he wants to control the oil. No, he wants to control the food. He already knows about the bees. He's keeping this quiet while he works on his invasion plans."

Chapter Forty

"How's dad doing?" Teresa asked her mother. "I've been trying to get through to you for three days."

"Sorry to keep you out of the loop, honey. Our cell phones don't work very well inside the hospital. Keep praying for your dad. We almost lost him a couple of times. The doctors are concerned about his head injuries," Marie told her daughter from the hospital cafeteria.

"I should come home right now and be with you,"

Teresa said.

"Your dad wouldn't want that. You need to finish out the semester."

"Do you know how hard it is to concentrate with dad all messed up. I feel so helpless," Teresa said.

"Michael and I feel the same way. There isn't much we can do right now except pray. We talked to your dad a while ago. He finally came out of the coma."

"What did he say?"

"He wasn't making any sense. He kept asking about the bees. He said they're all dying. It must be all the drugs they have him on."

"That's odd. I was just watching CNN and they were reporting about how the bee population is getting dangerously low," Teresa said.

"Your dad is sharing a room with another patient and the TV is on constantly. He probably heard something about the bees while he was unconscious."

"How are you holding up, mom?" Teresa asked.

"I'm a mess. I don't know what to do. Your dad made me promise that if anything ever happened to him, I'm to reach out to his cousin Richard, the doctor. His cousin is out of the country on a mission to immunize babies in

Africa and I don't want to interrupt him. I just don't know what to do."

"Mom, you need to stay strong. Dad is going to get through this. We're all going to get through this. I have a great support group of girls in my dorm and each one is taking turns praying for dad in the chapel. I'll ask them to pray for you, too, for wisdom and strength."

"I can't believe all this is happening. Your dad was almost home. We were so excited to start fresh here in Iowa. His car is totaled. I don't have a job. We don't even know where we're going to live. Thank God the health insurance is still active," Marie said.

"Calm down, mom. God has this. You have your entire family around you. Just take this one day at a time. Okay?"

Marie started sobbing uncontrollably. "I don't know what I'll do if your dad doesn't make it."

Marie's phone started beeping. "Wait a minute honey, I'm getting a text message from your brother."

Marie read the message, *Dad's waking up. Come quick.*

"Teresa, I need to go. Your dad is waking up. Keep praying. I'll update you soon."

"Love you, mom," Teresa said before she hung up.

* * *

Marie pulled out a Kleenex and wiped the tears from her eyes. A stranger sitting at the end of the table walked over and put her hand on Marie's shoulder.

"Are you okay, ma'am?" the woman asked in a soft voice.

"My husband hit a deer on the I-80 and we're not sure he's going to make it. He was unconscious for three days. He woke up for the first time a couple of hours ago and then went back to sleep. I need to get back to him. My son said he's waking up again."

"I'm a volunteer here at the hospital. My name is Hope. Let me know if there's anything I can do for you."

"I've been praying for hope for three days," Marie said.

"Here I am in the flesh," Hope said, offering a handshake. "I'll be your angel."

"Thank you, Hope. I'll see you again. Thank you. I just needed a little shot in the arm. I've got to get back to my husband."

Marie darted out of the cafeteria and headed for the elevator. Moments later she was back in the room.

"Dad's been asking for you, mom," Michael said as soon as he saw his mother enter the room.

"Marie, are you here?" Thomas asked.

* * *

"I'm right here, honey," Marie said, taking his right hand in hers.

"Has the war started yet?" Thomas asked.

Marie snapped at Michael. "I need you to change the channel on that TV. It's giving your father nightmares. No more CNN. Tell the patient."

Michael walked over to the other patient in the room and asked about changing the channel while Marie comforted her husband.

"I wish I could see you, Marie," Thomas mumbled. "It's so dark with these bandages on."

Michael yelled out from the other side of the curtain, "hey mom, I found the HGTV channel. Is that okay?"

"Perfect. Thank you. Your dad will love it."

"Very funny, Marie. You know I can't see anything. I could care less about TV right now."

"But Thomas, you're having nightmares from all that news crap on CNN."

"No Marie, I'm not having any nightmares. I found the man in the mirror. I've been to the other side."

"Heaven?" Marie asked.

* * *

"No, it's not Heaven. It's a place like another dimension."

"Thomas, your head is messed up really bad. You are having nightmares."

"Listen to me Marie. I'm not crazy. Remember those ghosts you and Michael were seeing in California?"

"You mean the ones you told me weren't real?"

"Yes. *Those* ghosts. Bedrock told me they were from the spirit world. We woke them up when we added on to our home. We were living on top of a sacred Indian burial ground."

"Who the hell is Bedrock?"

"He's the man in the mirror. The caveman. He visited me when I got knocked out. He's one of my ancestors."

"And what does this Bedrock want with you?"

"He wants to help me."

"With what?"

"To find the lost ones."

"And who are they?"

* * *

"All the people who don't have a clue about Jesus coming back."

"You're not making sense, Thomas. Your body is loaded with all kinds of drugs and you have some serious brain injuries. Your own imagination is getting the best of you. This is one hell of a dream."

Thomas pulled his wife close to him. "Let me ask you one question, Marie. And you need to be honest with me. Okay?"

"What is it, Thomas?"

"My legs are gone, aren't they?"

Marie was silent.

"Marie, are my legs amputated?"

"How did you know this, Thomas? You can't see anything with those bandages on and we've never talked about this in front of you."

"Bedrock told me all about it. He told me what I have to go through in my recovery. I know everything that is about to happen. Like I told you the first time I woke up, it starts with the bees. And they're disappearing, aren't they?"

"I thought you were overhearing it on the news, Thomas. Yes, there's a problem with the bees. They can't pollinate any more. Too much genetic engineering."

* * *

"That's the first sign that Bedrock shared with me. Now, can you tell me if anything is going on in Russia?"

"What do you mean?"

"Are the Russians overloading their borders near Ukraine?"

"Yes."

Thomas nodded his head. "That's the second sign."

"Oh my God, Thomas. You really are having visions."

Dr. Rickets entered the room and interrupted the conversation. "How are you feeling, Thomas?" he asked.

"Drowsy."

"He knows about his legs, doctor," Marie said.

"I'm not worried, doctor. Just give me some of those blade runners like that Olympic runner used. I'm going to need them for all the home improvement projects once I find us a fixer-upper."

"We weren't going to tell you about the amputations until you were further along. That's the reason your bandages are still on. Would you like me to remove them?"

* * *

Thomas nodded his head.

Dr. Rickets pulled some supplies from the cabinet and went to work on the bandage removal, slowly cutting away at the layers of gauze.

Thomas opened his eyes for the first time since the accident. He noticed Marie and Michael staring at his head.

"That bad, huh?" he asked his family.

"I don't mean to scare you dad, but you look like one of the zombies from the Walking Dead."

"Well, maybe with my legs gone I can get a part on the show," Thomas joked.

Thomas closed his eyes and went back to sleep.

Chapter Forty-one

"Bedrock, I'm back," Thomas yelled. "Where are you?" His voice echoed. He waited several moments and raised his voice. "Bedrock, I need you."

Bedrock's image appeared as if he were beaming aboard in a Star Trek episode.

"Are you okay, my son?" Bedrock asked.

"I saw my body with no legs. My wife and son could barely look at me when the doctor removed my bandages. Then I woke up here and I was all alone. Where were you?"

"With my wife and son," Bedrock answered. "They are excited for all the people who will be crossing over soon."

"Slow down," Thomas ordered. "You're hitting me with too much information. Help me understand what's going on here."

"My wife, Chara, she knows what war is all about. It happened long ago when I left her to find work. The invaders came. They burned everything. They killed my Chara. They murdered my unborn son. When I returned home to tell Chara my good news about finding work, she was on her back with a sword in her belly. My village was still burning. All the men were dead and the women were gone, except for my Chara. I went into shock. My anger consumed me. I lost my soul."

Thomas interrupted Bedrock. "But you just told me you were with your wife and son when I called out to you. How can this be?"

"They are on the other side now."

"But you said Chara and your son were murdered."

"Yes. They were murdered. But they are past death now."

"Can you tell me what happened from the beginning?"

"When I came home and saw her on the ground, I knew my life was over. I lost control of my mind and my body. That's when the devils came. No more was I Bedrock. I was Legions, meaning multiple evil spirits. They owned my thoughts. I fled into the hills trying to escape these devils. The voices stayed in my head. Night and day I howled like a mad dog. Anyone who came close to me was in danger. The villagers in the area tried to lock me up but I escaped with broken chains dangling from my shackles. I tore my clothes from my body and lived in the wilderness. I scratched deep into my skin every time I heard my wife screaming for help. I wanted to die but the evil spirits refused to let go of me."

"I remember the first time I saw you in the mirror you looked like a madman," Thomas said.

Bedrock paused for a moment and took a deep breath. "The evil spirits let me see many things. I saw the future generations. I saw the wars. I saw you. None of my visions made sense to me. I only knew that my mind no longer belonged to me. It belonged to the dark spirits. Until I met the man in the white robe who came to rescue me from the other side of the Sea of Galilee. He heard my cries and he came. I knew who he was the first time I saw him. The spirits inside of me knew him, too. And they ordered my legs to run away from him. I fixed my eyes on him and froze like a statue. I watched him and his followers hike up the rugged hillside to reach me. My heart was about to explode right out of my body. Then my mouth started moving and words were shooting out from inside of me. I yelled at the top of my lungs, 'Son of the most high God, why do you torment me?'"

"Why did you ask that, Bedrock?" Thomas asked.

"Because the dark spirits tricked me into believing God ordered my village to be wiped out. Now, standing in front of me was my enemy. But I was wrong. It was all because of the dark spirits. They did not tell me about free will. They did not tell me Jesus came to make all things new. That's when it happened."

"What happened?"

"Jesus ordered the devils out of my body. But they didn't want to back to the place where they belonged. So they begged the man in the white robe send them into the pigs. That's when my mind came back to me. I was free. I was new again. And I could see into the man's heart. I knew him. I knew where he was from. I knew everything. I told him, 'master, please let me follow you. Wherever you go, I want to follow you.'"

Thomas asked, "Did you follow him?"

"No. He wouldn't let me. He told me I knew too much. Even more than his followers who were with him for three years. They were weak. They couldn't do anything without Jesus. They had no idea this man was the Son of the Most High God. The spirits knew. They were with him. They thought they were better than him. They wanted their own kingdom and they wanted to be in charge. Then the war in Heaven broke out. It was Angel against Angel. The ones who wanted to be their own god were defeated. They roam the planet looking for souls who lost their hope, like me, Bedrock, the man with nothing but anger and hate. I was the perfect body for them to live in. I became their prisoner. Then Jesus changed everything."

"I don't understand why Jesus didn't let you follow him. He asks everyone to follow him," Thomas said.

"What time is it?" Bedrock asked.

"I have no clue, Bedrock. We're in the in-between, whatever the hell that means. There aren't any clocks here and you're asking me 'what time is it?'"

"What time of the year is it?" Bedrock asked.

"Spring," Thomas replied.

"And what are you getting ready to celebrate?" Bedrock asked.

"Until I hit the deer and got my legs amputated I was getting ready to celebrate my new life in Iowa," Thomas said.

Bedrock slapped Thomas across the face. "You're disrespecting your elders. Knock it off. Try again. What is the world getting ready to celebrate?" Bedrock asked.

* * *

"Easter," Thomas answered.

"And what is Easter all about?" Bedrock asked.

"The Resurrection."

"Now we're getting somewhere, my son of many sons," Bedrock said. "Jesus told me that if I stayed with him I would stop the Crucifixion. Jesus was safe with his followers. They were all dense. They were ready to run at the first sign of trouble. Not me. I had been through Hell. Jesus didn't need warriors, he needed lame people. I needed to be as far away as possible when the time came to put Jesus to death. He asked me to stay behind when he went home."

"That must have been really difficult for you," Thomas said.

"What kept me going was that he told me he would be back. He did come back one more time before he went to the other side. He visited just before they crucified him. The crowd of people waiting for him was one of his largest ever. He came back without his apostles to see me one more time. Everyone was waiting for him because of me. That's why he named me Bedrock, which means the invisible one."

"What a story," Thomas said.

"Yes. I was the publisher for all the people who weren't Jewish."

* * *

"But you didn't have publishers 2,000 years ago."

"I was the publisher of stories by the mouth," Bedrock said. "And you have my DNA. I can tell you every member of your family from my time to yours who published stories, mostly about the wars. And the greatest is about to happen."

"You're fading again, Bedrock."

"Yes. They're calling you from the other side. Go back to your family."

Bedrock disappeared.

Chapter Forty-two

The alarm bell on the heart rate monitor woke up Marie and Michael. Thomas was shaking uncontrollably. He thrashed his head from side to side. The two jumped from their chairs and rushed over to see what was going on.

"Thomas, you're having a bad dream. Wake up," Marie shouted.

Thomas sprang up from his hospital bed. "Where's Bedrock? Where did he go?"

* * *

Dr. Rickets rushed in to check on Thomas. The nurse was right behind him. Marie was the first to speak.

"He's having another nightmare, doctor."

"Don't worry, Mrs. Morgan. It's normal for patients to go through these episodes," the doctor said.

"I'm not delusional," Thomas shot back.

"Calm down, dad," Michael said.

"I am calm," Thomas said.

"That's not what all those machines are telling us," Marie interjected.

Dr. Rickets made some notes on the chart and asked the nurse to bring Thomas some medicine to help him sleep. "Your blood pressure is elevated, Thomas. I'm going to give you something to calm you down. How are you feeling?"

"I wish I could take all of you to the place where I just came from," Thomas said.

"You need to go back to sleep," the nurse said. "I'll be right back with something special to help you."

The doctor's pager started vibrating. "Thomas, I'm needed down the hall. I'll be back to check on you later. Get some rest." Dr. Rickets grinned at Marie and

Michael and told them not to worry about Thomas before leaving the room.

"I'm worried about you, Thomas," Marie said once the doctor was out of the room.

"You don't need to be worrying about me, Marie," Thomas said. "But there is something you can do if you want to help me."

"What is it?"

"I need a Bible?"

"Why? Thomas, are you dying?"
"Not today, Marie. I need to check on something Bedrock told me."

"Dad, your Bible is in the car. Do you want me to get it for you?"

"Yes. And hurry. I won't be able to stay awake once that nurse gives me my medicine."

Michael kissed his mother and gave his dad a thumbs up sign before departing for the hospital parking lot.

Marie leaned down and looked directly into Thomas's eyes. "You look really beat up, my love," she said.

"I don't have time to think about my looks right now, honey," Thomas said. "Right now I need to figure out what I'm supposed to do with all the information Bedrock gave me."

"Right now you're supposed to be resting and recovering from your accident. You're going to give yourself a heart attack."

Thomas grabbed Marie and pulled her closer to him. "Marie, there's some serious stuff going on right now on the other side."

"You're dreaming, Thomas."

"So you think I made up the bee story, huh?"

"You heard things while you were unconscious."

"And World War III? Was that something I heard on the news, too?"

"No one is talking about World War III, Thomas."

"Well, Bedrock knows about what's going on. It's all about to explode."

"What else did this Bedrock character tell you, Thomas?"

"He told me about the pigs."

"Did they cry wee, wee, wee, all the way home?"

* * *

"Stop making fun of me. No, Marie. They didn't cry wee, wee, wee, all the way home. They squealed, snarled and hurled themselves right over a cliff into the Sea of Galilee and drowned. Every single one of them. Bedrock was an eye witness. He saw the pig heads bobbing in the water. There were about 1,000 dead pigs. As soon as Michael gets back with the Bible I'm going to show you.

The nurse returned with a couple of pills and a cup of water.

"Nurse, can I please wait a little while before I swallow these pills?" Thomas asked.

"Sorry, sweetie. Doctors orders. We need to get your blood pressure down right away."

Thomas swallowed the pills and took a drink of water.

"Night, night, Thomas," the nurse said before leaving the room.

A few moments later, Michael walked in with his dad's Bible.

"Thanks, son," Thomas said. "Give it to your mother."

"What am I looking for?" Marie asked, opening the Bible.

"The pigs, Marie. Find the pigs."

Thomas closed his eyes while Marie thumbed through

his Bible.

"Can you narrow it down, honey?" Marie asked.

"New Testament. Find the story about Jesus crossing the Sea of Galilee with his apostles. I remember reading the pig story when I was a kid." Thomas drifted back to sleep.

"Your wife needs to turn to Luke. She'll find the pigs in chapter 8, verses 26-39."

"Bedrock, you're back."

"I never left. You're the one who decided to leave me right in the middle of our conversation."

"Bedrock, my family thinks you're part of my imagination. They don't believe anything I'm telling them."

"Ask your wife and son if the ghosts they saw in California were real or fake. Then, ask them to research the bee story I told you about. Have them get on a computer and check out Google Maps for the Karakoram super highway in China. Ask them where the highway ends. And when they tell you the highway was extended through Pakistan a couple of years ago, ask them why. Ask them what's going on in Ukraine. They need to look at all the maps of the area. The time bomb is ticking. China and Russia are getting ready to make an alliance. They want to destroy Israel. These are not your silly dreams or nightmares. These are the facts. And nobody in your home state is talking about Monsanto and how they went too far with their genetic engineering. You are going to be living next door to them when you recover from your accident. This is the epicenter of World War III. The battle will be to control the world's food resources. There won't be anymore corn once all the bees die. This is happening right now."

"So you're telling me you are the same caveman who met Jesus 2,000 years ago."

"Yes."

"And we are related?"

"Yes."

"But you said your son was murdered."

"Caleb wasn't my only child. After the crucifixion, I moved north. I settled in Ireland. I took a second wife in my old age. We had a daughter together. She grew up to be a mighty warrior. Her children became royalty. They ruled in Ireland for hundreds of years."

"And you expect me to convince my family that everything you're telling me is true?"

"That is your destiny."

"I'm not a fighter, Bedrock."

***

"Neither is Jesus. But He's coming."

"When?"

"Only the Father knows. But the signs are there. The prophecies don't lie."

"I need more than bees a cockamamie highway."

"It's the Karakoram Highway. And you already have more. You have me."

"There's a problem here, Bedrock. I'm the only person who can see you. Everyone is going to blame my visions on the accident. I'm not even sure you're real. Maybe this whole thing is some kind of crazy nightmare."

"Your legs are gone, aren't they?"

"Yes, they're gone."

"And who told you about that? The doctor? Your wife? Your son?"

"You told me, Bedrock."

"And how did I know?"

"How?"

"Because I see everything on the other side of the

mirror. My son of many sons, you need to prepare for the coming."

"How?"

"First, you need to convince your family that I am real and that you are from me. Then you need to teach the world about Jesus."

"And how am I going to do that?"

"We will talk about that when the time is right. You have some rehab to go through. You need to learn to walk again. That's all the time we have for now. Goodbye, my son of many sons."

Chapter Forty-three

Thomas opened his eyes and saw Michael staring at him. "Dad's waking up again," he shouted at his mother who dozed off in her chair across from Michael, her Bible moving up and down as she breathed in and out. Marie sat up and grabbed her Bible.

"We found the pig story, honey. We've been waiting for you to wake up so we can talk with you about it," Marie said.

"In the gospel of Luke?" Thomas asked.

"Yes," Michael and Marie said in unison.

* * *

"Did you know Luke was a doctor?" Thomas asked.

"We can't keep up with you, Thomas," Marie said. "You're drifting in and out of consciousness. You're sending us on a Bible trivia quest. And what you need to be doing is recovering from your accident."

"May I see your Bible, Marie?" Thomas asked.

Marie handed it over. Thomas tried fumbling through the pages to find the pig story but everything was blurry. He looked over at his wife with a befuddled stare.

"What's wrong, Thomas?" she asked.

"I need my glasses."

Michael reached over and pulled the Bible away from his dad.

"Let me read the story to you, dad," he said, turning to the story about the caveman. While he read the story, Marie took Thomas's hand and caressed it.

"Bedrock is the caveman," Thomas declared. "He's my ancestor."

"Is that where you get your craziness from?" Marie asked.

"It's where I get my warrior spirit," Thomas shot back.

"And Michael, too. Don't you remember when Michael was growing up how he always wore military fatigues and played with toy guns? And my dad, the marine? We are all descendants of this caveman Luke is writing about."

"His name is not written in the Bible, Thomas. I still think you're seeing things because of your accident."

"Marie, I started seeing Bedrock in the mirror when we were in California. That was *before* the accident."

"Dad, I don't understand why you never believed us when we told you our house in California was haunted," Michael said.

"Bedrock told me our home was on an ancient burial ground and the ghosts you saw were their spirits. We disturbed their graves when we added on to our home."

"So a ghost is telling you about other ghosts," Marie said.

"Bedrock told me you wouldn't believe me. I was wrong to not believe in your ghosts. I'm sorry."

Marie shrugged her shoulders. "So you won't believe the woman you've been married to all these years but you'll listen to someone you're seeing on the other side of the mirror?"

"Marie, there's more to it than that. Bedrock told me about the bees. I didn't hear it on the news. I heard it from his own lips."

Michael jumped into the conversation. "Dad, I don't know how you can be talking to someone who died 2,000 years ago. They didn't even speak English then."

"I don't understand it either, son," Thomas said. "Bedrock has been watching us from the other side of the mirror for generations. Maybe he's picking up our language."

"And what are the odds we're related to him?" Michael asked.

"The world population back then was much smaller twenty centuries ago," Thomas said. "Most of us can trace our roots and find lots of connections to people from that time. And don't forget about his eyes. Bedrock has blue eyes. Most of the people living in the Middle East have dark eyes. I'm positive Bedrock is my ancestor. Everything he's telling me makes perfect sense."

"It sounds much more personal than that," Marie said. "It sure does look like this ghost is stalking you."

"He's not a ghost, Marie," Thomas scolded.

"Then what is he and what does he want?"

"He wants the same things he wanted when he met Jesus and got the demons exorcised from his body. He wants everyone to know Jesus is coming back."

* * *

"We know that, dad."

"Bedrock said things are accelerating on the other side. He said if we paid attention to all the signs there would be no doubt the time is near."

"You mean with the bees disappearing and the events in Russia?" Marie asked.

"Yes, Marie. And the events in China, too. And Iran. Everything is connected."

"What about China and Iran, dad?" Michael asked.

"They're a part of the story, too. There's a reason why the men outnumber the woman in China. They are the ones who will be a big part of World War III. They will be on the move soon, towards Israel, where it all started. And Iran will have nuclear weapons soon. They're building rockets that can reach the United States."

"I'm pretty sure your drugs are making you disoriented, honey," Marie said.

"My head is clear. Go ahead, Michael. You read along in Luke 8:26 - 40 while I retell the story."

Thomas recounted the pig story as if he were there watching the whole thing while Michael followed what was written. When he got to verse 40, he asked Michael to read it out loud.

* * *

"Now when Jesus returned, a crowd welcomed him, for they were all expecting him," Michael read out loud.

"That was 2,000 years ago," Marie said. "What does that have to do with today?"

"The Bible is a mystery, Marie," Thomas said. "It's the living word of God. Jesus works outside of time. There's no past, present or future. It's all jumbled together. Verse 40 is for us. Jesus is returning and my job is to do the same thing Bedrock did. I'm supposed to share the story."

Michael shook his head. "Dad, I think mom's right. How can you expect Jesus to take a man who almost died in an automobile accident, lost his legs, lost his mind and use *him* to tell the world he's coming back?"

"The same way he used twelve people who didn't fit in with society to change the world. And Bedrock would have been a lot more visible if Jesus would've let him follow him in the last days. Bedrock had to stay behind so he wouldn't stop the crucifixion."

"That's a pretty far-fetched story," Marie said.

"So you think Bedrock is part of my imagination?"

"You haven't given us any facts to back up anything you're telling us, Thomas," Marie said.

"Here's one for you, Marie. Bedrock told me we're

going to be living in a house right next to Monsanto."

"Now I know you're losing your mind, Thomas. We don't have jobs, you have no legs and your imaginary friend who you say lived 2,000 years ago is picking out a new house for us. With what money? Are we going to make a down payment with Monopoly money?"

"Jesus rose from the dead. He walked on water. He told Bedrock he was coming back and he did. He told the world he was coming back and he will. And everything Bedrock told me is coming true."

"When is all this going to happen, dad? When is Jesus coming back?" Michael asked.

"Bedrock doesn't know the day and the time. He only knows some big changes are coming.

He knows the dark spirits personally and he knows they're preparing for something very big. It's not just the world that's preparing, it's the those on the other side of the mirror. Bedrock says we need to prepare."

Chapter Forty-four

"Hello Thomas. I'm Dr. Meyers. Dr Rickets asked me to stop by and visit. Do you mind if I sit down?"

"Welcome to my luxury suite, doctor. This is my wife, Marie, and my son, Michael. Are you here to check out my legs?"

"Stop being such an ass, Thomas," Marie said, slapping him across the face.

"No, Thomas, I'm not here to check out your legs, I'm here to ask you some questions." Dr. Meyers shook hands with Marie and Michael before sitting down next to Thomas. "It might be better if we talk in private,

Thomas. Is it okay if your family steps into the waiting room until we're done?"

Marie kissed her husband on the forehead and Michael waved good-bye to his dad before leaving the hospital room.

"So doctor, are you a specialist?" Thomas asked.

"No, Mr. Morgan, I'm not. I'm a psychiatrist."

"So, you want to know how I'm feeling, huh doctor?"

"How do you feel, Mr. Morgan?"

"Please. You can call me Thomas. From the knee caps down I would say there aren't any feelings. You want to know how I feel about that, doctor?"

"That's a great starting point, Thomas. How do you feel about the double amputation?"

"Well, it's a hell of a way to lose twenty pounds, wouldn't you agree, doctor?"

"It looks like your sense of humor is still working just fine," Dr. Meyers answered.

"The jury's still out," Thomas said. "At least my family doesn't have to worry about me running away."

"Thomas, I'm interested in knowing more about your

hallucinations. Dr. Rickets tells me you may be having a reaction to the drugs you're taking."

"So, you think I'm hallucinating. Is that right?" Thomas asked.

"It's common for patients to see things when they're on the type of medication you're on, Thomas."

"And how do you explain the visions I had *before* the accident?" Thomas asked.

"I'm not here to explain anything, Thomas. I'm here to ask questions and observe."

"Fire away, doctor," Thomas said.

"How long have you been having visions?" Dr. Meyers asked.

"Six months."

"How were you feeling when you had your first vision?" Dr. Meyers asked.

"How would you feel if you saw a naked guy staring at you when you looked in the mirror, doctor?" Thomas fired back.

"Why do you think he wasn't wearing any clothes, Thomas?"

***

"The demons occupying his body drove him crazy and he ripped them from his body," Thomas answered. Dr. Meyers pulled out his notepad and jotted down some notes.

"So this naked man is crazy?" Dr. Meyers asked.

"That's the only way I can explain all the marks on his body."

"What marks?"

"The first time I saw him, his body was covered with bruises and deep scratch marks. He probably used his finger nails to claw into his flesh."

"Why do you think he did that?"

"To forget about his wife and unborn son."

"Why did he want to forget them?"

"Because they were both murdered."

"By whom?"

"The people who destroyed his village."

"Why did they do that?"

"I don't know," Thomas replied. "But they killed Chara when they found out she was pregnant. Bedrock was out looking for work when it all happened. He came back and everything was wiped out. That's when he lost his mind and got possessed by demons." Dr. Meyers added to his notes.

"So, this man you call Bedrock is visiting you when you look in the mirror?"

Thomas stared directly into Dr. Meyer's eyes and paused before answering. "You don't believe me, do you, doctor?" Thomas asked.

"I'm just trying to find out how you feel about all this, Thomas."

"Look doctor. I know how silly all this looks from where you're sitting. It's really not important how I feel. What matters is that you have proof my visions are real."

"I don't doubt you're having visions, Thomas," the doctor said. "And from your point of view everything you see while you're sleeping does appear to be very real."

"Doctor, you didn't hear me. I said I started having visions *before* the accident. The first time I saw the naked caveman in the mirror I was wide awake. The second time I saw him I was also wide awake. And the third time I saw him I was very much awake."

"Were you consuming any kind of drugs or alcohol?" Dr. Meyers asked.

* * *

"I had a couple of drinks *after* I saw Bedrock for the first time but not before. And no, I don't do drugs."

"How do you know his name?"

"He told me his name."

"Where is this Bedrock from?"

"Near the Sea of Galilee."

"As in Israel?"

"Yes."

"Has anyone else besides you seen this caveman?"

"No. I'm the only one."

"You said something about proof this Bedrock exists. What proof do you have?"

The nurse walked in to give Thomas his next dose of medicine before Thomas could answer. "Take these pills and swallow," the nurse said, offering Thomas a cup of water to wash down his medicine. Thomas followed her instructions and then turned back to Dr. Meyers.

"Dr. Meyers, I'm going to give you proof I'm not crazy and that Bedrock is real. The next time you see me you're going to believe everything I'm telling you, no matter how preposterous everything may appear. Before you leave the hospital, I want you to visit the restroom. Look directly into the mirror and flash a number between 1 and 1,000 using your fingers. Don't tell anyone else what your number is. This medicine the nurse just gave me is going to knock me out until tomorrow morning. I want you to come back tomorrow and I will give you proof that the caveman is real. Deal?"

"I will be making my rounds mid-morning and I will stop by to visit again."

"Promise me you will pick a number and flash it in the mirror. Write the number down and stick it in your pocket. I don't want you to play any games with me. If you don't have the number with you when you stop by, I won't let you back in my room."

"I'll see you tomorrow, Thomas. Yes, I'll pick a number for you before I leave the hospital. Thanks for letting me chat with you today."

The two men shook hands and Dr. Meyers walked out of the room. He headed over to the waiting area where Marie and Michael were sitting.

"What do you think about Thomas's condition?" Marie asked as soon as the doctor approached.

"This case is interesting to me because Thomas tells me his hallucinations started before the accident. I'm going to need to probe deeper before I can answer your question, Mrs. Morgan. Your husband tells me he can show proof that his hallucinations are real. His medication is powerful and it may be playing tricks on him. Your husband told me he won't see me again unless I do something for him first."

"What does he want?" Marie asked.

"I'm supposed to go in the bathroom and flash a number in the mirror using my fingers. Then, I'm supposed to write that number down and bring it with me tomorrow when I have my follow-up meeting with your husband."

"Are you going to do it?" Michael asked.

"Sure," Dr. Meyers responded. "It will build rapport with your dad, Michael."

"Thank you for humoring him, doctor," Marie said. "I just pray his head clears up and we can take him home soon."

"It's my pleasure, Mrs. Morgan. Please excuse me. I'm going to stop by the restroom and flash some numbers in the mirror before I go home."

Dr. Meyers stopped in the restroom and made sure no one was around before he peered into the mirror. He held up both his hands and put one on top of the other forming two circles that resembled the number 8. Then, he took his left hand away leaving the number 0. Finally, he made two more circles with both hands and put them on top of each other to form one more number 8. Next, he pulled out his notepad and a pen. He wrote the number 808 on his notepad, tore off the sheet of paper, folded it several times and stuck it in his wallet.

Chapter Forty-five

Dr. Meyers took a deep breath before entering Thomas's room. He stuck his hand in his pocket to make sure the folded up note was in place and he walked in. Marie was flipping through some pages in a woman's magazine she picked up from the gift shop at the hospital.

"Good morning, Mrs. Morgan. I came to check in on your husband. How are you doing today?"

"My husband has been sleeping all morning. He woke up screaming a few times in the middle of the night. They increased his medication to calm him down."

"Where is your son?"

"He's spending a couple of days with his cousins. I think he's getting antsy sitting in this hospital room every day without being able to get an internet connection. I just want to get my husband out of here and get back to some kind of a normal life."

"Today is going to be an important step for your husband. I think it may be a good idea to talk with him while you're in the room with me. I need to help your husband understand that his hallucinations aren't real. His brain is suffering from trauma and he is going to need your help in the recovery process. It appears he is having trouble sorting out what's real and what's imaginary. He may go into denial when I show him his visions aren't real."

"What are his chances for a full recovery, doctor?"

"Your husband has a loving family. That will play a vital role in the healing process. Much of his recovery is dependent upon how dedicated he is to rehab. There's no reason your husband can't lead a full and productive life. My focus here is to help him ease back into reality."

Thomas began stirring in his bed and opened his eyes. Marie walked over to him and leaned down to give him a kiss.

* * *

"Thomas, Dr. Meyers is here to meet with you and he asked me to stay. Is that okay with you?"

Thomas nodded his head and looked over at Dr. Meyers. "Did you pick a number, doctor?"

"Yes, Thomas, I did."

"And did you write it down as I requested? Thomas asked.

Dr. Meyers pulled out the folded up paper and shook his head yes.

"Can you please hand your note to my wife?"

Dr. Meyers handed over the folded up paper to Marie and then opened up his notepad.

"May I have a sheet of paper and your pen, please?" Thomas asked.

Dr. Meyers handed Thomas a sheet of paper and pen. Thomas scribbled something on the paper and folded it up. Then he handed it over to Marie.

"I need a drum roll," Thomas said.

"Stop being so dramatic, honey," Marie scolded.

"Okay, let's settle this. Marie, will you please open the doctor's note and read what number he wrote down?"

* * *

Marie unfolded the paper and read out loud. "808."

Thomas appeared expressionless.

"Are you okay, honey?" Marie asked.

"We have a psychiatrist with us, honey. I think you should get his opinion."

Dr. Meyers jotted something down on his notepad and then looked over at Thomas. "I think once your wife shares your number with us we will be able to begin the recovery process. I'm going to do my best to help you get back to reality. This exercise is a great first step. I'm glad you suggested it. Do you want your wife to share your number or should we just skip it?"

"I'm ready to go to work, doctor. I'm ready to face reality. Go ahead, honey. Share my number with Dr. Meyers."

Marie slowly unfolded the paper. Her face turned pale. Silence filled the room. She was frozen.

Dr. Meyers turned back to Thomas. Thomas's face was like a skilled poker player in a high stakes tournament.

"What's your number?" Dr. Meyers asked.

Thomas didn't answer. Instead he help up his hands. He held up eight fingers and paused. Then, he held up one hand and gestured a zero using his thumb and four fingers. Last, he flashed eight more fingers.

Dr. Meyers set his notepad in his lap and raised one eyebrow, like Mr. Spock from the Star Trek series.

"Fascinating," Dr. Meyers said.

Marie was the next to speak. "I always believed in ghosts but this is unbelievable."

"How did you do this, Thomas?" Dr. Meyers asked. "I made sure I was alone in the bathroom and I didn't share my number with anyone."

"It was Bedrock. He was watching you the whole time. We visited three times in the middle of the night. He shared a little bit more about what's going to happen. It scared the hell out of me."

"This changes everything, Thomas," Doctor Meyers said.

"Does this mean you no longer think I'm crazy?" Thomas asked.

"Your not off the hook yet, Thomas," his wife joked, trying to reduce the tension of the moment.

"It's the world that's on the hook, Marie," Thomas said. "You need to get me out of here so we can prepare."

* * *

"That will be up to Dr. Rickets. I'm going to meet with him right away about the latest revelation. I'll be back later to check up on you. I have a lot of questions to ask you about your visions."

Dr. Meyers closed his notepad and reached over to shake hands with Thomas and his wife. When he extended his arm, his hand was shaking uncontrollably. "I wasn't prepared for this," Dr. Meyers said.

"Neither was I," Marie added.

"Well, that makes three of us," Thomas said. "All I can say is the people on the other side of the mirror are preparing for something. It's big. It's really big."

Chapter Forty-six

"Are you okay, Larry?" Dr. Rickets asked.

"Thanks for seeing me on short notice, James. This is an urgent matter." Dr. Meyers responded.

"Have a seat and tell me what's going on," Dr. Rickets said.

"James, I just met with your patient, Thomas Morgan. It was a follow-up from our initial consultation yesterday. I surmised he was suffering delusions as a result of trauma to the head from the car accident. The patient insisted I test him to prove his hallucinations were real. I've never seen anything like it. He gave me proof this morning his visions are real."

Dr. Rickets scooted his chair closer to Dr. Meyers and asked, "What proof?"

"Proof that this caveman person he claims visits him while he's sleeping really exists."

"You've got to be kidding me, Larry," Dr. Rickets shot back.

"No James. Your patient insisted I look in the mirror and hold up a number. Then he asked me to come back and share the number. I did what he requested expecting to debunk his hallucinations."

"What happened?"

"We both picked the same number, 808. The odds of that are one in a thousand. But there's more. I was alone in the men's restroom. I used hand gestures to show my number, like this." Dr. Meyers demonstrated how he used his hands to make the numbers 808.

"Go on," Dr. Rickets said.

"The patient used the exact same hand gestures I used when I flashed the 808 in the mirror."

* * *

"So you're telling me Thomas Morgan is not delusional?" Dr. Rickets asked.

"I'm suggesting something beyond our current understanding is in play."

"I've known you for a long time, Larry" Dr. Rickets said. "And we have had some great discussions about religion. You are one of the greatest skeptics I know. It's so unlike you to be talking like this."

"James, I'm an agnostic, not an atheist. I deal with facts. What I'm saying here is that this is the first time I've seen evidence something is going on outside our level of awareness."

"You mean like doubting Thomas from the Bible?" Dr. Rickets asked. "The disciple who refused Jesus came back from the dead unless he could poke his fingers through the holes in his hands?"

"I doubt everything until I have proof. Your patient offered me all the proof I need to validate his claims that his visions are real. Mr. Morgan says there isn't much time. He wants to be released from the hospital."

"That's not going to happen, Larry," Dr. Rickets said with a somber look on his face. He pulled out Thomas's file and opened it up. "Take a look at this. We found this in the X-rays."

Dr. Meyers scanned the file. "Cancer?" he asked.

"I'm bringing in an oncologist to do more tests. That spot on his lung appears to be a tumor."

"Have you shared this with the patient yet?" Dr. Meyers asked.

"We weren't looking for this when the X-rays were taken. This discovery occurred about an hour ago and I was getting ready to visit the patient about it when you called. Would you like to be with me when I break the news to Mr. Morgan and his wife?"

"Yes, James. I want to be there. In fact, I would like to spend as much time as possible with Thomas to learn more about his visions."

"Great. You understand the human brain better than I do and I need your expertise to help the family cope with the prognosis. If you have time, we can meet with the patient right away."

Dr. Meyers nodded his head yes. Dr. Rickets picked up the phone and buzzed the receptionist. "Suzy, I'm going to be away from my desk for about an hour. Page me if any emergencies come up." The two doctors walked out together and headed over to Thomas's room, chatting along the way.

"I'm really glad you're helping out on this one, Larry," Dr. Meyers said as they headed for the elevator. "This Morgan guy is going to need to some serious counseling. I can't imagine the suffering he's going through. I don't know if I could handle losing my job, losing my legs, having visions about the world coming to an end and now finding out there's a spot on my lung."

"It could be worse, James. At least he kept his health insurance intact."

"He seems resilient. I just don't know how he's going to react when we tell him about the tumor."

"Do you want to tell the patient, Larry? You have a better bedside manner."

"You're his primary care physician, James. Why don't you talk and I'll back you up?"

Dr. Rickets opened the door and Thomas's room. Dr. Meyers followed behind. Thomas was playing cards with his wife. "Who's winning?" Dr. Rickets asked.

"Thomas. He has all the luck in the family. Would you like to sit down, doctors?" Marie asked.

"No thanks, Mrs. Morgan. Why don't you sit down while we go over some things?" Marie sat down next to Thomas.

"Mr. Morgan, I have some bad news to share with you. We took a closer look at your X-rays and found a spot on your lung. We need to run some additional tests."

* * *

Marie started sobbing. Thomas was unfazed. "Looks like my luck just took a turn," he said.

Dr. Meyers intervened. I'm here to offer counseling for you and your family as you deal with this crisis.

"Thank you, doctor. Your help is much appreciated. It doesn't look like I'm going to be able to leave this hospital any time soon. If you really want to help, could you please spread the word about Bedrock?"

"What do you need?" Dr. Meyers asked.

"Talk to the Pentagon. Let them know about the visions. Call the Pope. We need to tell the world what's going on. Tell them about Bedrock."

"Do you think they'll take my calls?" Dr. Meyers asked.

"The world needs to know," Thomas insisted. "Promise me you'll make the calls."

"I promise."

Silence filled the room. Thomas stared at Dr. Meyers. "What are you waiting for, doctor? Go make the calls."

Dr. Rickets handed a box of tissues to Marie and the two doctors walked out of the hospital room.

Chapter Forty-seven

"Stop crying, Marie," Thomas said, wiping the tears from her face with a tissue.

"This isn't fair, Thomas. I'm in shock."

"This is so small compared to what's about to happen, my love."

"A spot on your lung is small? Get real, Thomas. You have cancer."

"That's not what defines me, Marie. Neither do my

missing legs. What defines me is how I deal with the cards I'm holding. Yeah, it looks like a shitty hand. I really don't want to be here in this hospital bed. I'd rather be on a beach in Maui with you and the family. That's not going to happen."

"What are we going to do, Thomas?"

"We're going to fight. We have a head start. We know what's about to happen."

"About the cancer?" Marie asked.

"The cancer, too, Marie. But I'm talking about World War III. I'm talking about Jesus coming back. Yes, I'll fight the cancer. I'll do what I need to do to walk again. I promise you, I'm gonna walk out of here. I'm going bionic. Just order me some new body parts and I'll be on my feet again."

Marie stopped crying and reached out for Thomas's hand.

"You're my man, Thomas. I don't know where you get your strength from."

"Marie, it's thousands of years of good genes. Bedrock helped me understand who I am and where I came from. It feels good to know about my ancestors."

"This whole thing is so crazy, honey. A few months ago you wouldn't even acknowledge the ghosts haunting our home in California. Now you've convinced your doctors that your visions are real. What are we going to do when the media gets a hold of your story?"

"I'm not going to do anything. I'm stuck here in my bed. You're going to be my spokesperson."

"Hell no, Thomas. You know I'm shy. There's no way I'm going on the news."

"Just keep it simple, Marie."

"Everyone's going to think I'm crazy."

"You have Dr. Meyers to back you up. He already evaluated me and he knows I'm not crazy. He will help you mentally prepare. I need you, Marie. You can do this."

"But what about all the skeptics? They're going to attack us?"

"Who cares? The people who will listen can prepare and the skeptics won't matter."

"I'm scared, Thomas."

"Of what?"

"Everything's happening so fast."

Thomas stared at Marie with a stern look on his face.

"Look, Marie. God has a plan. Our job here is to cooperate. We are a part of the plan. Bedrock has been sticking around for 2,000 years to help us at this very moment. Yes, everything *is* happening fast. The bees are dying. The food supplies are going to dwindle quickly. The tanks are moving in Russia. China already started a cyber-space war with us. Iran is lying to us about its nuclear plans. It's going to escalate. And Jesus is going to show up during World War III in the same area where He freed Bedrock from his demons next to the Sea of Galilee."

Marie paused. She bowed her head and started crying again.

"What's wrong, honey?" He asked.

"It's Michael. He's been talking to a recruiter. He's planning on enlisting. I'm afraid for him."

"When did this happen?" Thomas asked.

"He decided while you were in California. Michael wanted to tell you when you got home. Everything changed when you hit the deer. He's joining the army."

"It's in his blood, honey. We knew this from the time he was a young boy. Remember all those army pajamas he wore? And the military back pack he carried around when it was 100° outside?"

"Yes, Thomas, I remember. The first books he read

were about Bible warriors. He always played with toy guns and the GI Joe's you gave him from your childhood."

"He's following in his ancestor's footsteps. I'm glad I found them when I was studying our genealogy. The Irish kings, Captain James Starkey, all of them were warriors. This is what Michael is supposed to be doing with his life." Thomas said.

"None of them were in World War III," Marie said. "Our son might die on the battlefield."

"Marie, he belongs on the battlefield. There's nothing to be afraid of. Remember what Jesus said about death? He conquered death. We have eternal life."

"I'm just having trouble knowing our son may be on the front lines. Your ancestors fought Indians and people with swords. Michael could face biological or chemical warfare. He could get nuked."

"The only person in our family who is getting radiation is me, honey. And the only fallout will be my hair."

"Oh God, Thomas, you are going to be a sight with a bald head."

"Let's just shave it off right now. We can tell Michael we're celebrating him joining the army."

"You've got an amazing spirit, Thomas. That's why I love you."

* * *

"Don't forget my sense of humor, Marie. I'm promising you this right now – no matter how tough life gets, I'm never going to lose my sense of humor."

"Oh yeah, that's all I need, a bald-headed Gallegher," Marie said.

"Put this on your shopping list, Marie. I need a shaver, some watermelons and a sledgehammer. We're going to have a party right here in this hospital room. Tell our friends."

Chapter Forty-eight

The man standing in the doorway flashed his badge and asked permission to enter. He was outfitted in a dark black suit with a skinny black tie and matching black hat.

"Are you one of the blues brothers?" Thomas asked.

"No sir, Mr. Morgan, I'm here to ask you some questions."

"Who wants to know?"

* * *

"That's classified, sir."

"How did you find me?"

"That's classified."

"I need to take a closer look at your badge," Thomas said.

Thomas studied the badge but it didn't reveal much. "Who are you working for?" he asked.

"I'm a contractor with the government. I handle investigations."

"Let me guess. Your investigations are classified, right?"

"Yes sir, Mr. Morgan. Can we get started?"

"Is the name on your badge real?" Thomas asked.

"It's the name that's been assigned to me."

"I'm going to call you Agent X, okay Mr. Investigator?" Thomas said.

The special agent pulled a notepad out of his black leather brief case and started scribbling some notes.

"How long have you been meeting with the informant?" Agent X asked.

* * *

"What informant are you talking about?"

"The man supplying you with information about the upcoming war."

"It's a long story," Thomas replied.

"Start from the beginning. Give me as much detail as possible," Agent X said.

"The informant's name is Bedrock."

"Is that a first name or last name?"

"That's the whole name. 2,000 years ago they didn't have surnames."

"Your informant is 2,000 years old? How can this be?"

"Maybe you can get your government buddies to figure that out. I have no idea. I'm not sure if he's dead or alive. Maybe it's something in-between."

"How did you meet?"

"He's on the other side of the mirror."

"Which mirror?"

"Any mirror. It doesn't matter which one. He can see me in any mirror I look at."

***

"Why does he visit you?"

"We're related."

"How do you know this?"

"Bedrock told me we're related."

"So he can see the enemy from any mirror?"

"Yes."

"I need to know what weapons the enemy is planning to use and where they plan to attack. Be as specific as you can."

"Bedrock told me there will be multiple attackers. He mentioned Russia and China. He talks often about the Sea of Galilee where he's from."

"So, this Bedrock can see the future?"

"Not exactly."

"Then how does he know we are about to enter World War III?"

"Do you ever read the Bible, Agent X?"

"It's been a few years."

***

"You may want to pull it off the shelf and dust off the cobwebs. All your answers are there."

"Point me in the right direction."

"You can find Bedrock in Luke's story, the one about Jesus casting out demons from the possessed man who lived near the Sea of Galilee. That's Bedrock."

Agent X filled up the pages with notes. "Where exactly in Luke?" he asked.

"Chapter 8, verses 26 to 40. It's right up your alley."

"What do you mean, 'it's right up my alley?'"

"The entire Bible is coded. Everything you seek is there. You're going to have a field day with the Book of Revelations. You have to read between the lines."

"And this Bedrock told you all this?"

"No. I figured that out on my own. What Bedrock did was tell me his story. It's all linked to meeting Jesus when he was possessed with demons."

"I studied the Bible in Sunday school, Mr. Morgan, and I don't ever remember a man named Bedrock."

"Here's the deal, Agent. Bedrock wasn't part of the inner circle. He wasn't Jewish. He wasn't even religious. My ancestor was a regular guy, just like you and me. He was married. He left his village to find work so he could take care of his pregnant wife. Her name was Chara. While he was away, his village was plundered. Chara was stabbed in the belly. The other woman were taken as slaves. When Bedrock returned, he found his wife slain and all his friends murdered. He went crazy. The demons took over his mind and drove him to the caves. That's when Bedrock met Jesus. Jesus got rid of all the demons. He sent them into the pigs and the pigs went crazy. The reason you don't know the whole story is because Bedrock is a true warrior. He doesn't back down, like the apostles did during the trial. Jesus told Bedrock to stay away because Jesus was afraid Bedrock would stand up and tell the accusers who Jesus really was. Jesus had to die. Bedrock wasn't part of the plan. He got left behind. Jesus asked everyone he met to follow him – *except* Bedrock."

Agent X was writing as fast as he could, not wanting to leave out any details. Then he asked, "Do you think Bedrock could have stopped the trial, Mr. Morgan?"

"Jesus had a strategy. It was simple – surround himself with a bunch of fisherman who had no clue about who Jesus was. The plan was working perfectly. Then, Jesus met Bedrock. Thanks to the demons who were inside Bedrock's mind, Bedrock had access to the supernatural. The demons knew exactly who Jesus was and so did Bedrock. Jesus needed Bedrock to stay hidden until after the Resurrection."

"Does Bedrock know when Jesus is coming back and is

this part of World War III?"

"No."

"But Bedrock does know about troop movements?"

"He knows more than that. He knows why the troops are moving."

"Tell me more," Agent X said.

"It's all about the food supply. Check out Monsanto. Their latest seeds have been over-modified. The bees can't pollinate. That's why they're disappearing. The Russians already know this. I bet our government knows, too. The Russians are nervous about what will happen when there's not enough food to go around. That's why war is eminent. Bedrock told me about the bees so I could convince people what's going on."

"So Bedrock wants this story to get out?"

"Yes."

"I can't let that happen."

"You told me you're here to investigate what's going on. I don't believe you. You're here to shut me down."

"I'm part of a classified operation, Mr. Morgan. I need to make sure the American people don't become hysterical. You're story could cause mass panic."

* * *

"My story could save a lot of people. Bedrock is reaching out because something big is about to happen. The American people need to know what's up."

"Who else knows your story?"

"My wife, my children, my doctors and some of the nurses."

"I've already interviewed your doctors. You need to stop talking about Bedrock immediately."

"And what will happen if I refuse?"

"You don't want to go there, Mr. Morgan. For the country's sake, I'm asking you to stand down."

"You know I'm not crazy, don't you, Agent X? You know Bedrock is real. Your presence here this morning tells me our government already knows."

"It's classified. And this meeting never happened. Thank you for your time, Mr. Morgan. Get some rest."

Agent X put his notepad back in his briefcase and walked out.

Chapter Forty-nine

"I've got some bad news for you, Thomas," Dr. Rickets said when he walked in to the hospital room.

"What else can go wrong now, doctor?" Thomas asked.

"It's your insurance. We admitted you because you were in a life and death situation. None of us are on your plan. This hospital. Me. Dr. Meyers. We're going to need to transfer you to another hospital."

"You've got to be kidding."

* * *

"I'm not. Our admin people have been working on this since we admitted you. An official from HSS was in my office earlier going over your case."

"I knew it. They got to you, didn't they?"

"What are you talking about, Mr. Morgan?"

"Someone from the government was here a while ago and he was asking a lot of questions about my visions."

"Did he give you a name?"

"He showed a badge. His name started with an Sh. He told me my case was classified and that I'm not allowed to talk to anyone about my visions. He also said he was going to shut you and Dr. Meyers up."

"Thomas, other than your wife, you haven't had any visitors today."

Thomas paused for a moment. He had a look of disbelief on his face.

"So, how often do you get HHS people visiting you at the hospital, doctor?"

"It's never happened before. Health care is changing dramatically. They want to control costs. Your case is part of cost containment. We're going to move you this afternoon. I came to say good-bye."

* * *

"What about Dr. Meyers? He evaluated me. He knows something big is about to happen."

"There was a family emergency. I got word about an hour ago he's catching a flight to the Washington, DC area."

"Look at me in the eyes, doctor. You know the truth about my visions. You know I'm not crazy. I probably should have died in that car accident. But I didn't. Angels were protecting me. Now I've got cancer. Both my legs are gone. But one thing remains. I'm determined to tell the world about Bedrock. I'm not going to let the government hush me up. Are you going to help me?"

"Mr. Morgan, I can't. There are privacy rules. Once you leave my care, you're no longer my patient. I'm forbidden to talk about your case with anyone except the doctors who are assigned to you."

"And Dr. Meyers, too?"

"This applies to all hospital staff. Dr. Meyers is not on your plan. I'm sorry. Our hands are tied."

"Where are they sending me?"

"I don't know the details. I'll make sure one of our staff members notifies you before the transfer takes place."

"Does my wife know about this?"

***

"She knows there are complications with your insurance company. You're the first to know they made a transfer request to a hospital that's in your plan."

"What transfer request?" Marie said, entering the room.

"They're moving me, honey," Thomas said.

"Mrs. Morgan, this hospital and the doctors on staff are not part of your husband's health insurance plan. Your insurance company is requesting us to transfer you husband today to a hospital that's in your plan," Dr. Rickets said. "Someone from our staff will be available to answer any questions you have. I'm sorry. I have to go now."

Dr. Rickets shook hands with Thomas and Marie and departed. Marie buried her head between her hands and closed her eyes.

"Marie, they're shutting me down," Thomas said. "I had a visitor from the government today. They know about my visions. That's why they're moving me out of here. They don't want anyone to know the truth."

"I believe you, Thomas. I've been on the phone all morning with the claims department. Something fishy is going on."

"Why do you think that?"

* * *

"All their questions were about your mental health. They never once brought up your cancer or your physical health. At the end of the conversation they told me if we want our coverage to continue we need to sign non-disclosure agreements – both of us."

"There was guy here earlier, Marie. He said he's from the government. He told me if we talk about my visions we'll be in serious trouble. He said my case is classified. They're moving me because they don't want this story to get out. Dr. Rickets said there's no record of any visitors today besides you. These guys are using dirty tricks. I don't like it one bit. I don't even know where they're moving me."

"What are we going to do, Thomas?"

"I don't know. Dr. Meyers knows my story is true. They got to him. He's out of the picture. Everyone else thinks I'm delusional, except for agent X. Who's going to believe me?"

The nurse walked in with a stack of papers for Thomas to sign.

"How are you feeling today, Thomas?" she asked, handing him the paperwork filled with sticky notes showing where signatures were needed.

Thomas looked over the documents. "Why is this non-disclosure request in here?" He asked the nurse.

* * *

"It's from your insurance company. All patients are required to sign it."

"I refuse," Thomas said, handing the clipboard back.

"There will be consequences," his nurse replied.

"You may be liable for all hospital bills and your transfer will be stopped. You don't want to mess with your insurance company."

"I'm going to report this to my supervisor," the nurse said, walking out in a huff.

"This is our chance, Marie. Let's get the Hell out of here."

"You really are crazy, Thomas."

"Go find a wheel chair. We're leaving right now." Thomas started ripping off all the wires attached to his body. The heart monitor flat lined and an alarm went off.

"Looks like I'm dead, honey," Thomas said. "Make sure the insurance company gets the final bill."

Chapter Fifty

Marie located a wheelchair at the end of the hallway and hurriedly pushed it back to Thomas's room. The nurse on duty was already in the room responding to the alarm that went off as soon as Thomas disconnected all the sensors.

"What do you think you're doing with that wheelchair, Mrs. Morgan?" The nurse asked.

"We're leaving," she responded.

* * *

"I don't think so, honey. Your transfer won't go through until your husband signs the paperwork."

The nurse reached for the disconnected wires and began sorting through them.

"That won't be necessary, nurse," Thomas said. "I'm outta here. Bring that wheelchair closer, Marie," Thomas said.

"I'm calling security," the nursed said, reaching for the phone.

Marie ripped the phone chord from the wall and got in the nurses face. "We're done here," she shouted. "Get the hell out of our way."

The nurse scowled at Marie and marched toward the door. On her way out, she turned around and yelled, "This is what happens when the moon's full. And it's Friday the 13th. Watch out people, the crazies are headed for the streets."

Thomas motioned for Marie to hurry up with the wheelchair. "We don't have much time, Marie. Help me get out of bed."

Marie scooted the wheelchair next to the bed and helped Thomas maneuver. His upper body was so weak he could barely squirm out of the bed. Marie got behind him and placed her arms under his arm pits. She pulled him off the bed with all her strength and Thomas settled into the wheelchair. The hospital gown covered his amputated legs. Marie tucked the bottom of the gown under Thomas's stubs and started pushing Thomas out of his room.

A voice blared over the PA system. "Security. Attention, security. Please come to the 5th floor immediately."

Marie wheeled past the nurses station and headed for the elevator.

"You can't leave," the head nurse yelled.

Marie kept pushing until she reached the elevator. Other patients were peeking out from their rooms to see what all the commotion was about. The elevator door opened and the couple entered. Several of the patients cheered as the doors closed.

Marie pushed the button for the lower level parking lot and the elevator began descending. "What are we going to do, Thomas?" Marie asked.

"Just breathe, Marie. Stay calm. We'll figure out a plan once we're on the road." The elevator doors opened and Marie pushed Thomas out. She made a beeline for their Ford Focus and pulled the keys out of her purse.

"Put me in the back seat, Marie," Thomas ordered. "And put something over me to cover me up."

* * *

Marie opened the door and slid the wheelchair next to the backseat. She got behind Thomas and hoisted him from the wheelchair. In one swift motion, she managed to place Thomas on the back seat. She folded up the wheelchair and shoved it into the trunk. Marie pulled out a blanket and unfolded it. She draped it over Thomas as two security guards approached.

"We're looking for a patient, ma'am," one of the security guards said. "Have you seen anyone down here?"

"No sir," Marie answered.

"Keep your eyes open for a patient in a hospital gown. His legs are amputated."

"Doesn't sound like he'll get very far," Marie said, starting her engine.

"Sorry to bother you, ma'am," the second officer said. "Have a nice day. And be careful. It's a full moon today and it's Friday the 13th."

"Yeah, I'm aware of that. This is the day all the crazy people come out. Good luck capturing your escapee."

Three unmarked squad cars pulled into the parking lot with their lights flashing as Marie backed out and headed for the exit door.

"Stay still, my love," Marie said. "We're almost to the exit. Don't move."

* * *

The security guard at the exit gate walked out of the booth and bent down to talk to Marie.

"Do you mind if I take a look in the back seat?" he asked.

"What are you looking for, sir?" Marie asked.

"A patient left his room without permission. His wife was seen pushing him in a wheel chair. You match the description of the wife."

"Can't you see there's no one but me in the car?"

"The patient we're looking for is an amputee. I need to check under the blanket."

Marie pushed the accelerator to the floor and busted through the gate, leaving the guard behind. The guard radioed for help but it was too late. Marie made a hard right onto the busy street and disappeared into the traffic.

A voice called out from the back seat. "Be careful driving, Marie. There's a full moon out and it's Friday the 13th. There's a lot of crazies on the road today."

"I know, Thomas. I'm married to one of them. Where are we headed?"

"Stop at the nearest ATM and get as much cash as possible. You will need to ditch your cell phone and make sure you don't use your credit cards. They're going to be looking for us. Let's get as far away from here as we can."

Chapter Fifty-one

Marie's phone beeped. She waited until she stopped at the red light before checking her text message. "It's Michael, honey. He's looking for us at the hospital."

"Throw your cell phone out the window, Marie. They're tracking us."

"But honey. We can't ignore our son."

"We're fugitives now. You need to ditch the phone."

* * *

Marie held the phone out the window and let go. The light turned green but she wasn't moving. The driver behind her honked at her to get her attention. "You can do this, Marie," her husband encouraged from the back seat. "Drive."

Marie snapped out of her daze and put her foot on the accelerator. She scanned both sides of the street, looking for a bank. She found one a few blocks down the road and pulled into the parking lot. "I'll be right back, honey. I'm going to get us some cash." Marie unbuckled her seat belt and got out of the car quickly. She headed for the ATM at the front door and tried to get some cash but the machine refused. The message read, *contact bank.* Marie pulled her bank card out of the ATM machine and walked inside to talk with a teller. Three people were in line ahead of her. She bit her nails as she waited impatiently. An elderly gentleman in front of her noticed her nervousness. "You look like you're in a hurry, ma'am. Would you like to move ahead of me? I've got all day."

"Thank you, sir. Yes, I'm in a rush and my bank card's not working."

The teller at the end signaled for Marie and she walked up to make a cash withdrawal.

"Your ATM isn't working," Marie said. "I'd like to withdraw $500 in cash."

"I need to see your ID," the teller responded.

* * *

The teller called her supervisor.

"What's wrong?" Marie asked.

The supervisor typed something into the computer and turned to Marie.

"I'm sorry, Mrs. Morgan. Your funds have been frozen. A hold has been placed on your account. Let me make a phone call and see if I can get to the bottom of this."

"That won't be necessary. May I have my driver's license back, please?"

Marie grabbed her bank card and driver's license and headed out of the bank. When she opened the door she noticed a squad car with flashing lights pull in directly behind her parked car. Two officers rushed out and drew their guns. Marie ran toward the vehicle.

"Stay back," one of the officers yelled. A second police car arrived on the scene moments later with sirens blaring.

"Don't shoot," Thomas yelled from under his blanket in the back seat. "I surrender."

One of the officers opened the back door and pulled the blanket down. "What happened to your legs?" he asked.

"Car accident," Thomas replied.

***

"You're not authorized to be on the streets, sir," the officer said.

"Are you going to arrest me?"

"No. We're going to get you back to the hospital."

The officers in the second squad car attempted to disperse the large crowd gathering on front of Thomas.

"That's my husband," Marie shouted.

"I'm sorry ma'am. You need to stay back. We have orders to secure your husband."

An ambulance pulled up next to the second squad car and stopped. Two paramedics got out and headed for the rear of the ambulance. They opened the back door and pulled out a stretcher. Once they approached Thomas, one of the paramedics opened a passenger door and went in to check on Thomas. We're going to take you to the hospital, sir. Are you feeling okay?"

"I'm a prisoner of war," Thomas replied.

The other paramedic was standing outside and heard Thomas. He looked at one of the police officers and whispered, "mental patient."

Marie watched as the two paramedics hoisted Thomas out of the back seat and moved him onto the stretcher.

Once Thomas was loaded into the ambulance, they drove off.

"They're going the wrong way," Marie said. "The hospital is in the other direction."

The four officers on the scene got back into their cars. "You will be contacted soon," one of the officers told Marie before they drove off.

"I don't have a phone," Marie yelled. She stood next to her car all alone. The elderly man who let Marie go ahead of him inside the bank walked over to comfort her.

"It looks like you're having a rough day. Don't worry. The world's not going to end."

Marie paused for a moment and responded. "There's a lot to worry about. And I'm sorry to inform you that the world *is* going to end."

Chapter Fifty-two

Marie sobbed uncontrollably. The ambulance disappeared as quickly as it appeared. The elderly gentleman from inside the bank remained with her while the crowd dispersed. "What do you mean about the world coming to an end?" He asked.

"My husband knows something," Marie replied. "That's why they're locking him up. The people at the top are hiding the facts."

"What facts?"

* * *

Marie wiped her tears and cleared her throat. "Sir, what you just witnessed here is our government overstepping their authority. We are all losing our freedom. They're afraid of mass panic. I'm surprised they didn't lock me up, too."

"Who's afraid?"

"This goes all the way to the president. He pretends he doesn't know anything but they have ears everywhere."

"I'm not following. What does this have to do with your husband?"

"He knows things."

"What things?"

"About the end of the world."

"How does he know?"

"He's been in contact with someone from the other side."

"What other side?"

"It's like some kind of other dimension, a parallel universe."

"I heard one of the cops say he's a mental patient," the

man said.

"Do you believe in ghosts?" Marie asked.

"Yes," he answered.

"Have you ever seen a ghost?" she asked.

"No."

"Then why do you believe in them?"

"Because things happen that I can't explain."

"Exactly," Marie said. "And there's a whole bunch of things going on right now that can't be explained except by some kind of supernatural forces. My husband has been in contact with some kind of ghost who keeps appearing to him. Our military people are trying to use information from this other dimension to their advantage. It's wrong. They have no right to lock my husband up against his will. He's got cancer and he lost both his legs in an automobile accident. All they care about is how to contact my husband's source."

"So you think they are trying to get some kind of military advantage from accessing another dimension?" the man asked.

"Definitely. Who sends out the national guard just because someone wants to leave the hospital early? These people are relentless. I don't trust them. I don't even know where they're taking my husband. They asked us to sign confidentiality statements at the hospital but we refused. They were planning on moving my husband to some kind of secret facility but I got him out of there. That's why they came after us."

"What are you going to do?"

"I'm driving back to the hospital to get my youngest son. Then I'm going to find out where they took my husband. It's a long shot but I think I need to contact the media and get them involved."

The man took out a business card and handed it to Marie.

"Your name is Harold?"

"Yes ma'am. And you can call me anytime if you need someone to talk to."

"I'm sorry, Harold. I never introduced myself. I'm Marie. Marie Morgan. My husband's name is Thomas."

"Maybe I'll see your story on the Six O'clock news," Harold joked.

"If you don't then you'll know they got to me, too," Marie responded. "I threw my cell phone out the window when the cops were chasing me. I'll keep your card and contact you if I need anything."

***

Harold hugged Marie and walked her to her car. He opened the door for her and waved good-bye as she backed out and drove away. Marie turned on the radio and searched for a country music station to calm her nerves. A man's voice interrupted the broadcast. *We have an update on our top news story of the day. A mental patient who made a dramatic escape from a downtown hospital has been located and is now in custody of the authorities. Earlier, his wife plowed through a barricade and fled the hospital with her husband, a double amputee who is being treated for serious head injuries from a recent car accident. The man has been identified as Thomas Morgan. He was rushed to the hospital two weeks ago after striking a deer alongside Interstate 80. The man is suffering from delusions related to the car accident and hospital authorities noted he posed a threat to our town when he fled the hospital in a dangerous emotional state. The wife, Marie Morgan is wanted for further questioning.*

Marie turned off the radio and drove back to the hospital. She noticed a news crew in front of the hospital. They were interviewing the attendant from the parking garage on live TV. Marie drove back into the parking garage undetected and parked her car. Her hands were shaking as she turned off the ignition and got out of the car. She walked up to the main registration desk.

"Hello. My name is Marie Morgan. I heard on the news you have some questions for me."

"Hold on," the clerk at the desk said, picking up the phone. "I'll get someone who can speak with you."

Chapter Fifty-three

"Where are you taking me?" Thomas asked.

"A secure facility," the paramedic sitting next to him responded.

Thomas lifted his head up and strained his neck to look out the window and get his bearings. His upper body was strapped tightly to the stretcher and his arms were immobile. The ambulance zipped through the traffic at high speed. The loud siren made it difficult to carry on a conversation.

"What kind of secure facility?" Thomas pressed.

* * *

"It's top secret," the paramedic replied.

"What do you want with me?"

"It's classified."

The paramedic injected Thomas with a shot and Thomas became drowsy instantly. He closed his eyes and nodded off. When he woke up, he was back in the fog.

"Can you hear me, Thomas?" the voice asked from the mist.

"Where am I?"

"The other side of the mirror. Your body is on it's way to a government location that's off the grid."

"Why?"

"It's because of me."

"What have you done?"

"Exposed the truth."

"So why does the government care?"

"They're looking for a way to win World War III."

"It hasn't even started yet."

* * *

"It started. All the signs I gave you when we met. They came true. And the government has been spying on us. They know about me and they're using you to find me."

"I don't get it," Thomas said.

"They have specialists assigned to track down all leads related to the end of the world. They know the Book of Revelations better than anyone. They have special access to world-wide phone calls and emails. They even tracked down your genealogy. They found the connection between us. They know I'm your ancestor."

"And they know you're the crazy man from the Bible who was possessed?" Thomas asked.

"Yes. And they're going to probe your brain to look for a way to access any information about me that will help them win the war."

"This is freaking me out," Thomas said. "What can I do?"

"Nothing. These people don't have any control about what is about to happen. They think they do and they will try anything to gain an advantage."

"Bedrock, are you safe?"

"I'm already dead, my son of many sons. These people can't do anything to hurt me."

* * *

"But, what about me?" Thomas asked.

"That's a different story. They're going to probe you, prick you, interrogate you, even torture you."

"I'm so angry, Bedrock. I almost got away."

"You weren't even close, Thomas. You're wife's vehicle had a homing device on it. One of your legs has a chip in it near the spot where it was amputated. They always knew exactly where you were from the moment you left the hospital."

"Why didn't you warn me?"

"I didn't want to scare you."

"You're too late. I'm scared out of my mind. Will I ever see my wife and children again?"

"I don't know. These people will stop at nothing to keep their secrets away from the public."

"What do you mean?"

"Everything going on in the world today is connected. Benghazi. The IRS scandals. The troop movement in Russia. Hamas. Everything is tied to the end of the world. I see things escalating on this side of the mirror. Michael, the archangel, he's readying battalions of angels."

* * *

"For what?"

"For the King of Kings."

"Jesus?"

"Yes. Jesus."

"And the time is now?" Thomas asked.

"The time is near. Only the Father knows exactly when. But Michael and his angels need to make sure you don't blow yourselves up. Thermonuclear war is not good for the planet or for the people."

"What exactly is going on?"

"Prayers are being answered."

"Whose prayers?"

"The people who are being asked to renounce their faith. They are being slaughtered. Your government knows all about it but they do nothing. They're afraid to stand up to the terrorists."

"But they're not afraid to make me a hostage," Thomas said.

"Only because they believe you can help them."

* * *

"Should I help them?"

"You don't have a choice. Don't worry. I'm going to be here. You can tell them everything about me. It will be easier if you cooperate. They will be waking you up soon. Stay strong, my son of many sons."

Bedrock disappeared. Voices in the distance were calling out from beyond the fog. "Thomas, wake up."

Chapter Fifty-four

"He's waking up now. Shall I turn on the recorder, sir?"

"Yes, please. Are the electrodes secure?"

Thomas opened his eyes and squinted. A bright light from above his bed shone directly into his eyes. A series of probes were attached to his head and upper body. Thomas tried to lift his hands to block the light but they were bound at the wrists with hospital restraints and locked to his bed.

"Do you know why you're here?" a white-haired man wearing an ivory jacket and thick eyeglasses asked, peering into Thomas's eyes. The man's eyes appeared over-sized and startled Thomas.

"Yes, I do," Thomas replied. "You're looking for a way to win World War III."

"Are you recording this?" The man asked one of the others standing next to him.

"Roger."

"Let's begin. Mr. Morgan, we were hopeful you would sign the papers so your transfer to our facility would take place without any fuss. You have information that the government needs to protect its citizens. We have a right to use any means necessary to gain access. You will no longer have contact with the outside world."

"For how long?"

"I'm not at liberty to discuss that right now."

"What are all these wires for?" Thomas asked.

"We're probing your brain for your memories and we're recording them."

"But you don't have my permission."

"We don't need it. Your cooperation would be most helpful."

* * *

"Do I have a choice?"

"Not really. Please keep your head still."

A young lady sitting behind a large monitor adjusted the controls on her keyboard. "We found the region of the brain containing his memories, sir," she said.

The man gave a thumbs up to people in the room and then put his index finger over his mouth. "I need everyone to remain quiet now. It's time. Thomas, I want you to think about the man who has been supplying you with information about the world events. Close your eyes and recall your first meeting."

The three other people in the room walked over to the monitor and stared at the screen while Thomas complied.

"What do you remember?"

"I was packing boxes in my bedroom. I was in California."

"You're doing a great job, Mr. Morgan."

The computer screen revealed images of an over-size master bathroom and a large jacuzzi tub separating the bedroom and bathroom. Thomas's reflection from the mirror above the double sink was vivid. He was wearing a powder blue San Diego Chargers jersey and a pair of jeans.

* * *

"Thomas, where is your contact?"

Thomas looked around the room. Boxes were piled up everywhere. The bathroom window was open. Birds were singing. A gentle breeze filled the room. He turned back to the mirror and saw Bedrock. Thomas's pulse rate jumped. The men moved in closer to get a better look at the image on the computer screen.

"It looks like some sort of portal opening up in the mirror," one of the men whispered.

The interrogator looked over at the other men and reminded them to be quiet.

"You're doing a great job, Thomas. Describe what you see."

"It's Bedrock."

"Take a look at his surroundings. What do you see?"

"There are clouds in the sky. I see some boulders. I'm not sure, but it looks like he's staring into a pool of water."

"How do you know this?"

"Because the sun is on top of him and it's reflecting sunlight onto Bedrock. I can see the water ripples moving across Bedrock's face."

The interrogator looked over at the monitor and saw

the man's face for the first time. His hair was matted and overgrown and his cheeks were scarred. His eyes had an eerie Charles Manson stare. The questioner had to look away.

"What's happening now, Thomas?"

"I hear my wife calling me. She's making lunch."

The portal in the mirror closed. Thomas could see himself standing in front of the mirror. His hands were shaking and drops of sweat were rolling down his face.

"Honey, lunch is ready. Do you want to take a break?" Marie's voice echoed in the room where everyone was standing. Suddenly, Thomas was on a Hawaiian beach, laying on a striped beach blanket. Marie was handing him a sandwich from her picnic basket. She was wearing a turquoise one piece swim suit.

"Who's that sexy lady?" One of the men asked, ogling the image on the screen.

"Quiet, please, you're distracting Thomas."

"That's the day I asked her to marry me," Thomas said.

"Does this have anything to do with your caveman?"

"Not at all. Can't I have any privacy?"

"Shut it down, Nancy. That's all for now. Let's give

Mr. Morgan some time to rest. Clear the room please."

Thomas looked at the man in charge. "I don't even know your name."

"I'm Sam. We're going to be spending a lot of time together. You did great for your first session. Go ahead and let your mind wander while the monitor is off. When we come back I want you to block everything else out and concentrate on the caveman, okay?"

Thomas nodded his head yes. Sam was the last person out of the room. Before he left, he turned off the bright light shining in Thomas's eyes.

"Thank you, Sam."

"Thank *you*, Thomas. You're going to save a lot of lives." Sam closed the door and left Thomas alone. His mind drifted back to the day he proposed to Marie.

Chapter Fifty-five

Thomas heard a noise from the corner of the room and opened his eyes. A young woman was shuffling some things around on a cart she pushed into Thomas's room while he was still sleeping.

"Who are you and what are you doing?" Thomas asked.

"My name is Claire. I'm here to serve you breakfast and help you get ready for the day."

"How am I supposed to eat with my hands chained to

my bed?"

"I'm going to feed you. How are you feeling today, Mr. Morgan?"

"How would you feel if you were locked up and your family was taken away from you? I'm soaking wet from my accident in the middle of the night. It would have been nice if someone had been around last night to help me get to the bathroom."

"I'm so sorry, Mr. Morgan. I didn't start my shift until an hour ago. We have strict instructions to keep you secure. I'll see what we can do moving forward so there are no more accidents. Let me get you cleaned up."

Claire lifted up the sheet and got busy cleaning up the mess.

"How did you lose your legs, Mr. Morgan?"

"Traffic accident. I hit a deer and ended up it a ditch. I don't know if I'm lucky or unlucky to be alive."

"Why do you say that?"

"Look at me. I'm a prisoner. My insides are loaded with cancer cells and I have more wires coming out of me than my home entertainment center. I don't even know what day it is or what time it is."

"It's 4:30 AM and today is Friday. The team will be

starting in a half hour. Are you hungry? I made you some oatmeal."

Claire added some milk to the oatmeal and grabbed a spoon from the cart. "Here you go, sir," she said, giving Thomas one bite at a time.

Sam was the first of the crew to enter the room. "Good morning, Thomas. Good morning, Claire. Are we ready to get started?"

"The patient wasn't able to properly relieve himself, sir," Claire answered.

"Mr. Morgan was supposed to have a catheter in place yesterday. Claire, please get this taken care of before we start our session. Anything else?"

"Yes, there's something else," Thomas said. "How about you let me talk to my wife and children before you start probing me again?"

"That's not in my control. There are bigger priorities right now, like setting up our defenses. War is eminent. We don't have time to be worried about small talk."

The rest of the team entered the room and took their positions. Claire finished hooking up the catheter and rolled the cart out of the room. Nancy was the last crew member to arrive.

"We're ready for you, Nancy," Sam said. "Go ahead

and turn on the monitor and let's start recording."

Sam pulled out his notepad and began asking a series of questions.

"Thomas, you told us yesterday about your first meeting with Bedrock. I want you to close your eyes and go back to that encounter. Can you remember any more details?"

Thomas closed his eyes. Claire's image popped up on the monitor. Nancy giggled. "He must have a thing for blondes," she said. "Good thing she's not here to see these images. Where did those high heels come from? I don't recall her wearing those when she checked in this morning."

"Concentrate, Thomas," Sam said. "I need you to think about Bedrock."

Claire's image faded and the screen went black for a moment. Bedrock re-appeared, this time wearing a white robe and a pair of sandals. He was standing upright, completely motionless.

"What do you see?" Sam asked.

"It's Bedrock. He talking to me."

Sam checked the monitor. "I don't see his lips moving, Thomas. How is he talking to you?"

* * *

"We're in some kind of mist. I can hear his thoughts," Thomas replied.

"Tell me more about your memories," Sam said.

"These aren't memories. I see him right now."

The room erupted. Nancy was stunned. She turned to Sam. "This is impossible. Our probes were designed to record memories, not real time events," she declared.

Sam seemed unfazed. "Thomas, I want you to ask Bedrock if he knows why we're here."

Thomas paused. Bedrock moved his head from left to right and then stared straight ahead. "Bedrock knows," Thomas said.

"What's he telling you?" Sam asked.

"He's saying, 'do not worry, my son of many sons.'"

"What else does he have to say?"

Two sets of numbers flashed on the monitor... *32.8333...35.5833*.

"Ask Bedrock what the numbers mean, Thomas," Sam ordered.

An image of a giant lake popped up on the screen.

* * *

One of the men watching the screen pulled out his cell phone and entered the numbers in his web browser. "I know the location. Those numbers are map coordinates. That's the Sea of Galilee – 32.8333° North and 35.5833° East."

"Nice work, Jim," Sam said. "Oh my God, Nancy, this is mind boggling. Is the recorder getting all this?"

"Yes, Sam. All the images are coming through fine. These are all real-time projections."

Pictures from all over the world flooded the screen. They resembled satellite images. Each one appeared with map coordinates.

"Get the Department of Defense on the phone. Tell them we're making progress. I need someone in the lab right away," Sam shouted.

Thomas's body began convulsing.

"Shut it down," Sam ordered. "Get Claire back in here to help Thomas. He's on overload. Let's take a break."

Chapter Fifty-six

"What happened?" Thomas asked. Claire wiped the sweat from his face.

"You had a seizure, Thomas. Your body went into a series of convulsions. You had us all worried. Do you remember anything?"

"Yes. Bedrock told me not to be afraid. The others were asking him questions. My head started spinning. I blacked out."

* * *

"Your brain couldn't process the information fast enough. We got everything on tape. Our people are processing the information right now. Your country is thankful for all you're doing to help."

"Is that how my country thanks me, by chaining me to a bed and turning me into a porcupine?"

"This is for your own good, Thomas. You're in a top secret location and you're safe in this room."

"What's next?"

"We're going to give you some medicine to calm you down before we resume. Take this." Claire offered two pills and a cup of water for Thomas to swallow. "We're going to get started as soon as your blood pressure returns to normal." The rest of the team was busy reviewing the recordings from the first session. Sam was busy making a list of questions for the next round. A man dressed in a black suit and dark tie entered the room and walked over to Sam.

"Who's he?" Thomas asked Claire.

"I've never seen him before," she answered.

"I cleared my calendar and got a flight over here as soon as I got the news, Sam. Good work."

"Thanks, Tim. We're communicating with our subject in real time now. You're just in time for our second session."

"Is it okay if I have a few words with Mr. Morgan?"

"Please allow me to introduce you," Sam said.

"Mr. Snargel, this is Mr. Morgan. And this is Claire, Mr. Morgan's personal nurse."

"You can call me Tim. I'm with the Department of Defense. On behalf of the country, Mr. Morgan, I want to thank you for all you're doing to help us out."

"You can call me Thomas, sir. It's nice to meet you. I've seen you on TV before."

"I've seen you, too, Thomas. Sam and his team sent me the video from your meeting with your contact on the other side of...what is it? a mirror?"

"Yes sir, Tim. Bedrock resides on the other side of the mirror."

"And he claims to be one of your ancestors, correct?"

"Can't you see the resemblance?" Thomas asked. "Except for me having no legs, we're like twins."

Claire interrupted, "his blood pressure is normal, Sam. We can move forward anytime."

Tim reached out to shake Thomas's hand. Thomas reached as far as he could before the restraint held him back. "Looks like I'm a captive audience," Thomas joked.

"I got off the phone about a half hour ago with the president and he told me to say thanks for your service. This mission, code-named *operation caveman in the mirror,* is going to play a major role in the outcome of this conflict. Thank you, Mr. Morgan."

"Ask the president when I get to see my wife and children, Mr. Snargel Then maybe I won't feel like such a prisoner."

"Deal, Thomas."

"Are you ready to meet our caveman, Tim?" Sam asked.

"Let's roll," Tim said, offering a thumbs up.

Chapter Fifty-seven

"Relax, Thomas. Go to your happy place. Turn on the recorder, men," Sam instructed. Claire smiled at Thomas and grabbed his hand. An image of a young woman appeared on the screen. She was on her back in a hospital bed and appeared to be in agony.

"Who is that?" Snargel asked.

"It appears to be one of Thomas's memories. I believe the woman is about to give birth. I don't see a doctor in the room," Sam said. Thomas was mumbling. "Just breathe, Marie. Haa, hee, haa, hee."

* * *

A doctor rushed into the scene and the nurse stepped out of his way. Seconds later, the baby's head emerged with it's eyes already opened.

"It's a boy, Thomas shouted from his bed, shaking his restrained arms. His name is Patrick."

The men operating the equipment observed Thomas cutting the umbilical chord. "Isn't he handsome?" Thomas asked.

"I can't believe what I'm seeing," Tim said. "The image is so clear."

"We've been working on this technology for a long time, Mr. Snargel," Sam said. "It looks like this is our subject's happy place. His wife looks adorable. Look at her holding their baby."

"I'm loving this but my time is short with you and I'd really like to meet our caveman," Tim said. "Can we move on?"

The scene lingered on the screen. Marie handed the baby over to Thomas and he held Patrick in his arms for the first time.

"Where is Bedrock?" Sam hollered. The image faded. Claire put her hand on Thomas's forehead and whispered in his ear, "let's go find Bedrock."

* * *

A giant lake appeared on the monitor. A group of men at the lakeside were entering a small boat. Several hundred objects were bobbing up and down in the water.

"What is that?" Tim asked.

"Dead pigs," one of the men in the group uttered.

"Is Bedrock there?" Tim asked.

"Bedrock wanted you to see this," Thomas said. "It's one of his most important memories."

"Who are those people getting in the boat?" Tim asked

"I count thirteen men, sir," another technician said.

Some numbers flashed on the screen.

"Sir, those are the same numbers we saw earlier. That's the Sea of Galilee."

"Jesus Christ," Snargel said. "Oh my God, that's Jesus Christ in the boat."

The room got quiet. The men on the monitor sat down in the boat and paddled off while the pigs floated around them.

"Wait until the world sees this," one of the men declared.

* * *

"Gentlemen, let me remind you this is a top secret project. No one except the president of the United States is going to see this," Snargel said. "Am I clear?"

"Yes sir," the group responded. Tim turned to Thomas. "You're doing very well, son. I need you to ask Bedrock some questions. Okay?"

"Bedrock is standing by, Mr. Snargel. What do you want to know?"

"Ask Bedrock if He knows who those men are on that boat."

"Bedrock says you already said his name," Thomas responded. "That's why Bedrock is reaching out. He want's the world to know about what's about to happen."

"Son, we're in the United States of America. It's not my call to let the world know. I need our military to know and we need to be ready. Understood?"

"Bedrock says Jesus is not of this world and neither is he," Thomas said.

"What about the enemy?" Snargel asked.

"Bedrock says the enemy is all around us, just like they were in those pigs. The enemy once lived in Bedrock's head. The picture you see on the screen is the first image Bedrock saw of the world after Jesus cast the demons out of him."

* * *

"Does Bedrock know what the enemy is planning?"

"World War III."

"When?"

"It's already begun. You have the coordinates of the key positions. Bedrock gave those to you yesterday. There's just one problem, Bedrock says."

"What's that?"

"Many in our country have lost their way."

"No shit. That's why we need to build up our defenses."

"Bedrock has been watching us for 2,000 years. He said the reason Jesus is coming back now is because we are about to wipe mankind off the planet. The enemy is stronger than ever. For many, like Bedrock once was, the enemy is within."

"Demonic possession?"

"Yes. We all have our demons. Bedrock was forced to stay away from Jesus because he knew the truth. He had to stay out of the way. Jesus had to die so that we can be saved. Jesus was afraid Bedrock would intervene and talk the crowd out of killing Jesus. That's why Bedrock didn't get in the boat and follow Jesus. He had another job – to publish all the good Jesus did for him. Now that includes video publishing. You have the tape. It's not just for the president, it's for the world. The demons are going to do everything to stop you."

"What am I supposed to do?"

"Bedrock says you need to let me be reunited with my family."

"I'll see what I can do. My question is, 'how am I to prepare for what is to come?'"

"Bedrock says it would be a good idea to let our military men and woman have their Bibles back. Jesus is your best defense."

"Thank you, Thomas. You've done a great job today. Sam, get this over to my analysts. I'm on my way to meet with the president. Keep up the good work and keep me informed," Tim said, waving to the team before walking out of the room.

"Shut everything down, team. Let's give Thomas some time to rest. It's break time."

Chapter Fifty-eight

"Sam, Mr. Snargel asked to meet with you in private. He said it's urgent. He's waiting for you in your office," Nancy said.

"What's up?" Sam asked.

"He said to come alone."

Sam grabbed his legal pad and headed for the door. Thomas yelled out, "Don't forget to tell him I want to see my family."

***

"Just keep cooperating with us, Thomas and I'll see what I can do about your family. I'll be back soon, " Sam said before walking out of the room. He headed down the hallway and opened the door to his private office, a small room in the corner of the building. Tim Snargel was sitting on the couch that doubled as Sam's bed on long nights when he was too tired to go home. Tim stood up as soon as Sam entered the room.

"Nancy told me you've got an urgent matter to discuss," Sam said.

"Have a seat, Sam. I talked with the president about what I saw here today. We've got trouble."

Sam took a seat behind his desk. The top of the desk was cluttered and a stack of files was piled on top of an in-tray. There were sticky notes plastered all over the monitor on Sam's MacBook Pro which was on top of the desk with the laptop opened on the center of the desk. Sam slid closed the laptop so he could see Tim, now sitting in the chair in front of the desk. The sticky notes protruded from the laptop. Sam fidgeted. "What kind of trouble?"

"I'm the only Republican in the president's inner circle, Sam. And the truth is I'm not really in the inner circle. I've never really agreed about anything. I was against the surge in Afghanistan. It turns out I was wrong. I stood up when others wanted our soldiers to leave their Bibles at home so we wouldn't piss off the idiots who have the president's ear. Today was the straw that broke the camel's back. I told Hussein everything about what you're doing here. He wants to micromanage the whole project. And he told me loud and clear, 'No Bibles.' He doesn't believe the images you recorded today have anything to do with Jesus. I'm pretty sure he's being influenced by a group of people who are anti-christian. I also believe none of them have ever read a single page from the Good Book. Our differences are more than Democrat and Republican. He kept me on so he could look good. That shellacking at the mid-terms really got him mad. He's taking everything out on me. I'm the scapegoat. He's relieving me of my duties as soon as a replacement is found. He wants it done before his party gives up the Senate. You're the first to know. The rest of the world will know about my departure by prime time tonight."

Sam leaned in. "So, you're quitting?"

"That's a nice way of pulling a Donald Trump. I'm fired, but only you and my wife know that. I've got to play nicey, nicey in front the of the press and tell everyone 'it's mutual.'"

"What's going to happen to our mission?"

"The president has a lot on his plate. He wants war, not with the world but with my party. The whole immigration story is about distracting the American people from what's going on overseas. Operation Caveman in the Mirror is becoming a major headache for the president. If this story leaks, he's going to deny everything and blame it on me. This smoke and mirrors approach has worked well but the stakes are really high right now. You and your team need to be extremely careful. This can't get out to the public."

Sam scratched his head. "I'm going to miss you, Tim. You believed in me when I came to you for funding."

"You exceeded all my expectations, Sam. I'm really impressed with your work here. I just wish we could share this with the world. Maybe we could achieve some kind of peace in the Middle East."

"I can't take all the credit, Tim. There's something going on here I can't explain. The system was designed to access memories of the subject, not direct communication with people like Bedrock. And certainly not other people's memories. I mean, think about it. You and I just saw a scene from the Bible replayed right before our eyes and recorded for the president's eyes. He saw the tape, right?"

"Oh yes, he did," Sam replied. "And his inner circle jumped on it before he even had a chance to comment. They told him this is all some kind of elaborate hoax. They think my republican buddies are in on it, that it's some kind of right-wing conspiracy theory. That's why the president wants me out. He's listening to his friends. I'm sorry to have to leave you at such a critical time. It's not my choice. I believe in what you're doing."

"I don't see an easy way out, Sam. The entire Middle East is being purged of Christians. Israel doesn't acknowledge Jesus is the Messiah and Russia and China are doing everything in their power to bring us down. What would the world do if we shared today's video on Fox News? Who would believe us? Do you see what a challenge this is?"

"But we have proof," Sam said.

"Your first set of data is already being attacked. Some of the president's advisers believe the Chinese hacked into your system and they're playing games. They even believe Thomas Morgan is some kind of delusional psycho who needs help," Tim said.

"I don't know what to do," Sam said.

"What you do, Sam, is you get back to your team and you do everything in your power to glean everything you can from this Bedrock guy. He is an angel sent to us to help us win World War III. It's coming. You and I both know what we saw today is real. The rabbis knew who Jesus was. They had him put to death to keep their power. You can't kill Jesus twice. And I believe He's coming back. There are other things going on in the world that I'm not at liberty to share with you. It's all classified. Let's just say that what you uncovered so far confirms what I already know. That's why I dropped everything to get over here and see your project with my own eyes. I'm a believer."

Sam asked, "what about the Morgan family? Are they going to be able to be re-united?"

* * *

"We have a team watching them now. We're monitoring all their conversations. If anything leaks, the whole family will be thrown under the bus. I don't know if the president will give permission for them to enter this top secret facility. Not even congress knows this place exists."

"What should I do?" Sam asked.

"Remind your team to keep your mission classified. Wait for orders from the next person in charge. I wouldn't be surprised if the president himself visits you personally. I'll be dropping off the radar. You will be in my prayers, Sam. Keep up the good work. On behalf of the country, I offer my thanks. I have to leave now. The president summoned me back the White House."

"Good-bye, my friend," Sam said, shaking Mr. Snargel's hand. "And good luck."

"Thank you, Sam. You're a valuable asset. Good-bye. I'm praying for a favorable outcome."

Chapter Fifty-nine

"Are you Michael Morgan, son of Thomas Morgan?" the first man standing outside the door asked.

"Yes, sir," Michael responded.

"Is your mother home?" the second man asked.

"Yes, sir," Michael answered.

Both men pulled out badges from their suit pockets and flashed them briefly. "We're with the Federal Government and we need to speak with you and your mother. Please let her know we're waiting.

Michael closed the door and left both men outside. He rushed into the kitchen where Marie was preparing some turkey sandwiches for lunch.

"Mom, two men are at the front door. They're from the government. They want to talk to you," Michael said.

Marie wiped her hands and headed to the front door with Michael right behind. She opened the door. Both men flashed their badges. Roxy immediately lunged toward the open door and tried to get past Marie. Michael restrained her while she barked at the strangers.

"Ma'am, you and your son need to come with us right away," one of the men ordered.

"I'm not going anywhere until you tell me what this is all about," Marie said.

"It's classified. You are to come with us immediately. Please leave your cell phones and your personal possessions behind. One of our agents will remain here to keep your home secure."

"Can we eat our sandwiches first?" Marie asked.

"I'm sorry ma'am. There's no time to waste." a third agent walked up and showed her badge to Marie. "I've been assigned to secure your home. My name is Jennifer O'Neil," the 30 year-old agent said. O'Neil stood almost one foot taller than Marie. Her slender figure was covered up by her black military style outfit and black bullet proof vest.

"Help yourself to some sandwiches, Jennifer. I don't want them to go to waste," Marie said. Michael pulled his cell phone out of his front pocket and gave it to Jennifer. Roxy ran under the dining from table and continued barking.

"We'll explain everything on our way to the airport, Mrs. Morgan," the first man said.

"Do you guys have names or should I just call you the Blues Brothers?" Marie asked, making fun of their out-of-style thin black ties they were both wearing. "Do you guys both shop at the same stores?"

"These are our uniforms," the first man said. "Sorry to keep the conversation short but we have a plane to catch and they're waiting for us at the airport. Let's go," The two men escorted Marie and Michael to the black limo parallel-parked outside. The driver had the door opened for all four to get inside.

"I'm Mitchell and this is my partner, Lucas. We'll be accompanying you."

"How long is this trip gonna take?" Michael asked.

Mitchell's cell phone rang before he could answer the question. Mitchell looked at the number on the screen and showed it to his partner before answering.

"Agent Michell here," he said. "How can I help you?" The voice on the other end of the call was too quiet for anyone else in the limo to hear.

"Yes, sir, the package is secure. We're en route to the airport now. The limo entered the airport through a private entrance and drove over to a small jet parked next to the runway. The two men got out first and then signaled for Michael and Marie to get out. Mitchell walked up the stairs first, followed by Marie and Michael. Lucas pulled a small bag out of vehicle and climbed the stairs last.

"This is awesome," Michael said when he entered the jet. "I feel like I'm traveling with the Criminal Minds team."

"This is where our tax dollars go," Marie quipped. Michael and Marie sat down next to each other and the two agents sat down facing them. As soon as all four were buckled in, the jet taxied for take-off.

"When are you going to tell us where we're going?" Marie asked.

"It's somewhere where you two will be safe," Mitchell answered.

"Safe from what?" Marie asked.

* * *

"You will need to wait for your briefing, Mrs. Morgan. Sit back and relax. It's a short ride," Mitchell said.

"Do you know anything about my husband?" she asked.

"We're just the delivery people, Mrs. Morgan. All that is above our paygrade."

"What about my phone?" Michael asked.

"You'll get it back when all this is over," Lucas replied.

"Mrs. Morgan, your face is turning white. Are you okay?" agent Lucas asked.

Marie grabbed onto her son's hand and squeezed. "I really don't like flying," Marie answered. "Especially small planes."

"Don't worry, ma'am. You're safe with us. Let's talk about something to keep your mind off of flying. I hear your son enlisted. How do you feel about that?"

"Are you trying to give me a nervous break-down?" Marie asked.

"No. I'm just curious about your family." Marie was breathing so hard she looked like she was going into labor.

Michael jumped into the conversation, eager to share his excitement about joining the army. "My dad took me into the recruiting office while we were still living in California. Mom told me I could sign up for anything I wanted as long as it wasn't infantry."

"So what did you sign up for, Michael?" agent Lucas asked.

"Infantry."

Marie closed her eyes and squeezed harder. "That hurts, mom," Michael said. Marie didn't respond. Her knuckles were turning white.

"Tell me more," agent Lucas said, trying to calm Marie down.

"I was born to be a fighter," Michael said. "When I told my parents what I wanted to do when I grew up, the first they did was buy me a video, Black Hawk Down. They thought if I saw what war was about, I would look at other options. They were wrong. I watched that movie at least fifty times. I liked replaying the shooting scenes over and over in slow motion and I always imagined being there. Every night I dreamt about being transported in a helicopter to a war zone. I'm always one of the last ones left when I play against my friends on my X-Box."

Marie opened her eyes. "I don't know why my husband and I tried to interfere with Michael's plans. I thought we could change fate. The first time we put him on the monkey bars at age two, he flew across like a chimpanzee. We kept waiting for him to get tired. He just kept going, back and forth. Michael cried when we finally pulled him down. That's when Thomas looked at me and said, 'honey, I think he's going to be a Marine like his grampy.'"

"The marines tried to get me," Michael said. "They heard about my football and wrestling background from the army recruiter. When I went in the second time to sign up, the Marine recruiter was in the office next door and he told me it wasn't too late to sign with him. My sergeant walked in and told him to get the hell out of his office. I thought there was going to be a fight. When it came time to pick a job I went through my choices. Every job I asked about was filled up. Then he asked me, 'what about infantry?' I said yes, but. He picked up the phone and called in to see if infantry was open before I had a chance to explain about my mom's request. 'There's a spot open in infantry,' my sergeant said. I could feel my heart racing. The adrenaline was kicking in. At that moment I knew for sure infantry was my dream job. I told my dad first about my decision. He told me he would handle mom and not to worry."

"Thomas is doing such a great job of that, Michael, isn't he? We don't even know where he is. And he's dying. I can't afford to lose both of you." The jet hit an air pocket and caused all the passengers to jolt. "Geez. I don't even know if I'm going to survive this flight."

Agent Lucas tried to reassure Marie. "Nobody is going to die, Mrs. Morgan. And I think your son is going to be a fine soldier. I served four years in the army and it turned me into a man. I was infantry, too. My mama couldn't believe how much I changed when she came to see me graduate. I used to be really messy. I never made my bed. She about fell over the first time she came to visit when I got my own place, compliments of the GI Bill. The bed was perfectly made and all my belongings were neat and orderly. When I was growing up I never made my bed."

"When do you go to boot camp, Michael?" Agent Mitchell asked.

"I'm not sure, sir. I got an extension when my dad got in the car accident. I don't feel good about leaving right now."

"Do you have any siblings, Michael?"

"A brother and a sister. Patrick is thinking about the army after he graduates from college and Teresa is going to school in California. She's thinking about transferring so she can be closer to my mom. They've both been encouraging me to enlist and they believe it will help me get past all the bad things that are happening with my dad. I'm just glad we moved out of that haunted house in California."

"Let's not talk about the haunted house, son. You're going to scare these men," Marie said. "Besides, all that's behind us now."

"You're kidding, right?" Agent Lucas asked.

"No. Dad never believed us but we heard noises all the

time."

"Did you ever see any ghosts?" Agent Mitchell asked.

"The only one who ever saw anything was my dad. He never told us until after his car accident."

"I don't think we should be talking about that right now, Michael," Marie warned. "It's the reason why your dad is locked up. Let's not add to his problems."

The pilot signaled it was time for the final descent. Michael looked out the window while Marie sat in her seat with her eyes closed.

Chapter Sixty

"Mr. President, we're ready." Hussein was the last person to enter the White House situation room. He barely had time to get dressed before he was awakened at 3:00 AM to meet with his vice-president, Robinette Smiden, his secretary of state, John Forbes, his new secretary of defense, Westin Smarter, and four star General, Martin Dempsey, chairman of the joint chiefs of staff. The large circles under the president's eyes were evidence of his lack of sleep during the last three weeks of the escalating conflict. Hussein took a seat at the head of the conference table and looked up at the monitor.

"Mr. President, the images you see are from one of our drones circling above the north shore of the Sea of Galilee in Israel. It's now 10:17 AM in Israel. Three rockets were fired simultaneously at Israel by Iran one hour ago and they disappeared at the location you're looking at now," General Martin said.

"What do you mean, disappeared?" Hussein asked. "Were they shot down?"

"No sir, Mr. President. We detected no anti-missiles fired in response to the attack from Iran. They simply disappeared while we were tracking all three rockets."

"Why didn't Israel fire back?" he asked.

"I can answer that, Mr. President." John Forbes joined the conversation. "I was on the phone with Israel the moment we detected the missile launch aimed at Israel. Israel attempted immediate counter-measures. Everything stopped working. They are defenseless. They asked us to intervene. We can only observe the area from our drones. Our weapons cannot be fired inside their airspace."

"Who is doing this to us? How can this be? Is this some kind of cyber-attack?" Hussein asked the group.

"It appears to be some kind of shield. Nothing can go in or out of the area, except for our drones. We don't know who is responsible for this," General Dempsey said.

Hussein turned to Westin Smarter. "Welcome to the party, Westin. I guess this is your initiation. What are your thoughts?"

"Mr. President, we've always known the Sea of Galilee is important to the security of Israel. One of my teams is working on a theory right now but I don't have all the facts," Smarter said.

"I'll settle for a hunch at this point, Westin. Watcha' got."

"Jesus Christ," he answered.

Robinette Smiden put his hands in the air. "No swearing allowed here, Westin."

"I'm not swearing, sir," Smarter answered. "I'm speculating at the root cause of our weapon shutdown in the area. It's Jesus Christ."

"Oh, boy, the Muslim community isn't going to like this," Hussein said.

"You're right, Mr. President. They're not. We may be observing the second coming of Jesus Christ right here on our monitor," Smarter said. "We may not be able to fire any weapons in the area but somebody wants us to have a birds-eye view of what's going on. It makes sense if you follow what it says in the Book of Revelations."

"Refresh my memory, Westin," the president ordered.

"It says every knee shall bow. The only way that can happen is if the world sees Jesus."

"I'm going to have trouble selling this," Hussein said.

"You don't have to sell anything, Mr. President. All the major networks are reporting about the rocket attack from Iran. They're already calling in to get confirmation about our weapons shutdown. The story is already out there," Smiden said, after reading a text message from one of his advisors.

"I'm not going with your Jesus theory, Westin. You're doing a great job hitting the ground running but you're a little far-fetched on your theory. Let's look for something else. I'm sure we can come up with something that the public will buy. Anyone got any ideas about what we should say at our next press conference?"

"Mr. President, I think we're better off not saying anything. Any lie we put out there right now will only inspire the press to dig deeper. Besides, our enemies are watching the news coverage as well. Let's not tell 'em we're defenseless," John Forbes said.

"I agree, John," Hussein said. "Martin, do you have any guys on the ground in the area besides our drones?"

"Yes, Mr. President. We have a seal team in place on the north shore of the Sea of Galilee. We put them there at Snargel's request before he resigned."

"Okay. I don't want the press to know about our seal team. I do want to know everything about this shield and why the Israeli's can't fire any weapons. How big is the affected area?" Hussein asked.

"At least 8,000 square miles, sir," General Dempsey answered. "That's pretty much the entire geographic area of Israel. Their country's missile defense system is disabled. We are still monitoring the neighboring countries to ascertain the status of their military. Other than the three rockets fired by Iran, there haven't been any other incidents."

"So you're telling me our number one ally in the Middle East is completely defenseless and all we have to investigate the crisis is a seal team and some drones?" Hussein asked.

"Up until 3:00 this morning, Israel has always been able to take care of it's own defenses. They never gave us permission to bring in our own forces. We sent our seal team in without their knowledge or consent," General Dempsey said.

"Bibi's gonna blow a gasket if he finds out we're fishing around inside his country," Hussein said.

"He needs us, Farack. Maybe it's time you extend an olive branch to him," Smiden suggested. "I think you need to talk directly to him as soon as possible. We are on the brink of WWIII here. We cannot afford to let our enemies annihilate our number one ally. Don't you agree?" Smiden asked.

"John, you get on the phone with Bibi. Tell him we are behind his country 100%. Tell him we are moving more assets into the area immediately. Ask him what he needs from me. I don't want to talk to him directly. I'm still mad about the shenanigans he pulled when he tried to go around me to address congress," Hussein said. "Meanwhile, I'll get with my speechwriters and get something ready to say to the American people in the next few days. We'll try to keep everything quiet as long as possible. General, you stay close to the White House and keep me posted on the latest developments. If this really is WWIII in the making, I want to win this. Well, Westin, how does it feel to be meeting with me in the middle of the night?" Hussein asked.

"To be honest, Mr. President, I feel like I'm going to puke," the new secretary of defense answered.

"Now you know how I felt every time I met with your Republican predecessor, Westin. I'm glad I have you on my team. Just don't get too carried away with your Jesus theories," Hussein said.

"You got it, Mr. President. I'll report back to you as soon as I have more information.

Chapter Sixty-one

"Sir, radar has just detected three more rockets fired from Iran. We have a visual from one of our drones."

"Get it up on the screen. What's the target?" the commander asked.

"Same as the last one, sir. Israel."

"Time to impact?"

"90 seconds."

"Counter-measures?"

"Not enough time, sir. Israel has no defenses."

"Mother of God! Connect me with the Situation Room."

***

"Mr. President, we detected three more missiles fired out of Iran. All three will strike Israel in sixty seconds. We're sending you images from our drone. Mr. President, we have no assets available to assist," the commander said.

"What just happened?" Hussein asked. "We lost the picture over here."

"Our monitor just went dark, too, Mr. President. We have eyes on the ground. Connect me with Seal Team 3," the commander ordered.

"We've got them on the radio sir. Switching to speaker."

"Seal Team 3, what's your status?"

"This is Seal Team 3. We're in position at checkpoint 5. We were tracking three missiles. They're gone now."

"What do you mean gone?"

"They disappeared, sir."

"Were they intercepted?"

"No, sir. They vanished. There's no sign of them."

"Commander, we have ten more missiles. Same launch coordinates and same target. Impact in 90 seconds."

"I want that launch site taken down now," the commander ordered. "Mr. President, I say we go with our nuclear option."

"No, commander. Just keep observing," Hussein responded.

"We lost the missiles, commander. They disappeared at the same coordinates."

"Seal Team 3, what's going on?"

"We lost visual on the second set of incoming missiles. They vanished right in front of us. We don't know what happened," Seal Team 3 replied. "We're picking up something strange in the atmosphere directly above us. It appears to be some kind of a funnel cloud. There's no wind at our location but the clouds seem to be spiraling in fast motion around the funnel cloud."

"Copy, Seal Team 3," the commander replied. "Let's turn those drone cameras upward and get a closer look at what's going on."

Everyone in the situation room fixed their eyes on the large monitor. The drone cameras sent back images of the new cloud formations directly overhead moving counterclockwise at a rapidly accelerating pace. A gust of wind overpowered the seal team watching from their position below.

"This is Seal Team 3. We're encountering high winds. Visibility is dropping. The Sea of Galilee is getting choppy. It may be unsafe to extract us if the situation keeps deteriorating."

"Seal Team 3, this is Centcom. We have no plans to extract you. You are the only eyes we have on the ground in the area and we are relying on you for intel. We patched you in to the situation room so they can have real time updates. Tell us what's going on."

"The center of the vortex overhead is lighting up."

"Roger, Seal Team 3. We have it on our screen."

"The winds are getting stronger, commander. And white caps are forming on the water. Something's happening in the center of the cloud. There's a beam of light. It's shining down onto the surface of the Sea of Galilee approximately three hundred meters from our checkpoint. It's like a spotlight."

"I need a drone camera aimed at that spotlight," the commander ordered.

"Commander, there's a figure in the center of the spotlight. He's standing on the water with both hands raised up and he's wearing a white robe. The spotlight is retreating back into the funnel cloud. There's a series of explosions."

"Bombs?" the commander asked.

"No, sir. Trumpets. The figure is moving, sir. He's moving toward us."

The situation room erupted. Vice president Robinette Smiden was the first to speak. "It's Jesus. He's walking on water. His angels are announcing He's back."

"Slow down, Robinette," Hussein said. "This may be some kind of trick. Our enemies may be trying to distract us. This could be a projection or mirage. Remember when they did that in Planet of the Apes? It's mind control."

"Our enemies don't even know we're on the ground," Smiden said.

"The sea is calming down, commander," one of the seal team members said. "The wind stopped howling. The man on the water is standing still now. He's looking straight at us. He can see us. Our cover is blown, sir."

Chapter Sixty-two

"Welcome, Mrs. Morgan. I'm Lisa Cummings with the Department of Defense. This must be your son?"

"I'm Michael Morgan. Where are we? Is my dad here?"

"No, Michael. Your dad's not here. You're in a secure facility. We don't have much time. If you two will step into the conference room I'll tell you why we summoned you here. Agent Lucas and Agent Mitchell, will you please wait for us in the hallway? Follow me, please, Mrs. Morgan and Michael."

Lisa led Marie and Michael into a large conference

room with a TV monitor on the wall and directed the Morgans to sit next to each other at the conference table facing the monitor.

"Agent Jennifer O'Neil checked in about an hour ago. Your dog is doing fine. I wish I could say the same thing about your husband, Mrs. Morgan," Lisa said. "He's slipping."

"When are you going to let us see him?" Marie asked.

"I have permission to set up a video call with your husband. Before we begin, I need to fill you in on his health. We have the best doctors in the country helping him. Mr. Morgan is suffering from an aggressive form of cancer that has spread to his vital organs. There's not much we can do when it reaches stage IV. My boss asked me to get you here right away so that you can connect with him."

"Why can't we be with him?" Marie asked. "This is inhumane."

"I feel for you, Mrs. Morgan. The world is on the brink of war and we need your husband to help us out," Lisa responded.

"You're killing him," Marie said, reaching for a Kleenex at the center of the table.

"We're not killing your husband, Mrs. Morgan, the cancer is killing him. It's amazing your husband recovered so well from the double leg amputations and it's fortunate we found the cancer while he was under our care. I can assure you we have done everything possible to treat your husband. Is there anything I can offer you or your son before we initiate the video call?"

"No thanks. Let's get started. I really need to see my husband."

Lisa picked up the phone and dialed. "Sir, we're ready to connect. I have Mrs. Morgan and her son with me now. Can we begin?"

The video screen turned on and Thomas's image came into full view. An iv was hooked up to his left arm and a breathing tube was protruding from his nose. A series of probes and wires stuck out from his head. His eyes were closed.

"Thomas, your wife and son are on the televideo. Can you open your eyes and say hello?" his nurse asked, nudging him.

Thomas slowly opened his eyes and he lifted his head off the pillow to look into the monitor. His eyelids were heavy and he appeared groggy from all the sedatives he was receiving.

Marie cupped her hand over her mouth and stared at her husband. Tears welled up in her eyes. Michael spoke first.

"Dad, you look like a porcupine. What are all those wires doing sticking out of your head?" Michael asked.

"That's classified, son. I would tell you but then that pretty lady standing behind you will have to kill you."

"You're always the dramatic one, honey," Marie said. "I see your eyes are still working."

"It's so great to see both of you. I wish I could tell you I'm getting out of here soon but I'm all tied up at the moment." Thomas raised his left arm high enough to expose the wrist cuff attached to his hospital bed. "I guess these folks are scared you might break in here and pull another Houdini act with me."

"You're right Thomas. They're not going to let us near you. They won't even tell us where you are."

"Marie, I don't even know where I am. It really doesn't matter anymore. I'm so weak, baby. I keep having weird dreams. I don't know what's real and what's fake. Are you really on the screen, Marie?"

"Yes, honey. It really is me and Michael. We're here for you."

Thomas gazed into the monitor. "Son, I can't believe how much you've grown since I last saw you. I bet you're going to break 6' soon. You look great."

"Thanks, dad. I'm ready for boot camp. The army says I can wait for a while longer. They know about your accident."

"You stay out of trouble, son. Your mother can't afford to lose both of us."

"I don't want to lose you, Thomas," Marie said.

"Marie, you're not going to lose me. Not ever. You know I'm going to haunt you when I leave this place," Thomas said.

"That's not funny, dad. Mom and I are still recovering from our ghosts in California," Michael said.

"Well, I never recovered from mine, either. My ghost is with me every day."

Lisa interrupted from the back of the room. "Mr. Morgan, remember our agreement?"

"Yes, miss, I do. There are no ghosts, here. Right, nurse?"

"That's our story and we're sticking to it, Thomas," his nurse replied, winking at him from his bedside.

"Without breaking our agreement, let me just say if you ever want to know anything about area 51, you should ask these guys. They seem to have a lot of secrets around here," Thomas said.

"Sure, dad. Mom and I will just sneak in to wherever you are and we'll ask everyone all about area 51," Michael said.

"Stop it, you two. Michael, stop egging your father on. And Thomas, knock it off with your dry sense of humor. I can see where Michael gets his attitude from."

"All you need is one of these porcupine hats and we can be identical twins, son," Thomas said.

"You're a trend setter, dad," Michael said.

"Nurse, check please. I'm ready to go home, now."

"Sorry, Mr. Morgan, we haven't served dessert yet," his nurse responded.

"You see, honey. No respect. They never serve dessert here," Thomas said. Thomas put his hand over his heart and cringed. "I'm afraid I'm gonna do a self-checkout now, family. I love you." The heart monitor flat-lined and an alarm went off. Thomas slumped back into his bed and stopped breathing. Marie and Michael observed the commotion in the room. About a minute later, one of the doctors rushed into the room. He ripped open Thomas's shirt and reached for the defibrillator.

"Clear," he yelled, pausing before attempting to jump start Thomas's heart. The heart monitor beeped momentarily before it returned to flat line mode.

"Clear," he yelled again, making a second attempt with the defibrillator. Nothing changed.

The doctor looked into the monitor for a moment and saw the pain on Marie and Michael's faces. He pursed his lips and made one final attempt.

"Clear!" The monitor flat-lined. The doctor looked up at Marie and Michael and said, "I'm so sorry for your loss."

Marie grabbed her son and squeezed tightly. Lisa walked over and put her arms around both of them. "I'm so sorry for your loss, Mrs. Morgan. I'm so sorry Michael. May your dad's soul rest in peace."

Chapter Sixty-three

"This is a Fox News Special Alert. We just got word from our sources in the Middle East that Iran has fired two rounds of missiles at Israel. Both attacks were unsuccessful and there has been no response yet from Israel. Tensions are mounting and US troops are on high alert. We are awaiting word from the White House. President Hussein was wakened early this morning and is meeting with top aides including new secretary of defense, Westin Smarter, about the crisis. Iran has denied it fired any missiles and continues to deny it has nuclear capability. We'll have more for you after the break."

Chapter Sixty-four

Michael entered the men's restroom and walked over to the sink to splash water on his blood-shot eyes. He kicked the trash can with all his might and then pounded his right fist into the dry wall. "This sucks," he shouted.

Agent Lucas heard the noise and rushed in. "What's up, Michael?" he asked.

"He's dead. My dad's dead."

"I'm so sorry, buddy," he said. Agent Lucas's cell phone rang.

"Agent Lucas," he answered. "Yes, Michael's with me. We'll be out in a minute."

"Michael, we need to get you cleaned up. My boss

needs to see you. She's with your mother in the conference room." Agent Lucas helped Michael regain his composure and the pair headed back to the conference room. The two woman were sitting down at the table.

"Michael, there's been an accident at our house," Marie said. "Roxy slipped out of her collar while she was outside with agent Jennifer O'Neil. She ran out into the street. Jennifer chased Roxy but couldn't stop her in time. Roxy got run over. She's gone." Michael sat down next to his mother and put his head on the table. Marie reached out and massaged the back of his neck. The room was silent.

Chapter Sixty-five

"My son of many sons, we're together at last," Bedrock said, offering a bear hug to Thomas.

"What am I doing here?" Thomas asked.

"You have passed from your body," Bedrock answered. "You're in the in between now. You're free."

"I'm dead?" Thomas asked.

"You're better than dead. This is where the connected ones go," Bedrock said.

"Heaven?"

"Almost. Heaven is on the other side of the mist not far from where we're standing. I've been waiting in the in between for over 2,000 years for all my sons and daughters to come home. I will not enter Heaven until the last of my off-spring has passed from his body. Michael will be the last."

Thomas heard something from beyond. "Where's that noise coming from?" he asked. "I know that sound." The distant yelps grew louder and louder. A small critter clawed at Thomas's legs but he couldn't see through the dense blanket of knee-high fog floating around him. He squatted down and recognized his Chihuahua who was panting heavily after her long run. Roxy slathered his face with wet kisses and whimpered uncontrollably.

"How did she get her?" Thomas asked.

"She followed your scent. Your pet knew you were gone as soon as your last breath came out of your body. So she followed you. I have something else to show you, my son." Bedrock put his two index fingers in his mouth and whistled. The sound echoed and then disappeared in the distance. Two howls, one male and one female, answered back. Roxy turned to the howls and fired off a series of shrilling high-pitched barks.

"I must be dreaming," Thomas said, shaking his head in disbelief about what he was experiencing. Before Thomas could finish speaking, a large black and white animal lunged out of the mist and knocked Thomas on his back. A second brown and white sheltie jumped on top of Thomas and began licking his face. Roxy was spinning around in circles. Two more figures approached from far off.

The shorter of the two was dressed in a red suit with silver boots and silver gloves that nearly matched the color of the mist. He bent down and extended his right hand to greet Thomas who was still immersed in the fog.

"Nanu, nanu, my friend, I'm Robin Williams. Welcome. Would you like a hand up?" Robin grabbed Thomas and lifted him up off the ground while Lady, Lucky and Roxy sniffed at Robin's boots. The second figure raised his right hand and smiled at Thomas. Thomas had seen the familiar gesture many times. "I'm Leonard Nimoy. Welcome. May you live long and prosper."

Thomas pinched himself. "This is not logical," he said. "A short while ago I was chained to a hospital bed. Both my legs were amputated and I was grabbing at my chest but I couldn't feel my heart beating. Now I'm standing here with a ghost who has been haunting me ever since the time I lived in California. I'm surrounded by all three of my pets, two I buried in the backyard of my California home. I'm standing here with two of my favorite actors in the whole world who recently died.

Robin Williams asked, "Can we play rock, paper scissors to determine which of us you are happiest to see?"

"That would be highly illogical, Robin. Everything and everyone here is a ten. Every day here is your best day on earth increased by a factor of one billion. There are no comparisons. We are going to be with the Father soon. A day with the Father is like a thousand years and a thousand years is like a day. Our mission here is infinite and our journey is just beginning," Nimoy said.

Robin Williams looked at Leonard. "It's too bad you left your Spock ears behind, Leonard. Can you at least raise your right eyebrow for me? I love it when you do that."

Nimoy complied. Then, he did his Spock gesture one last time. "Live long and prosper, my friends."

"We're off to see the Wizard," Robin said. "You should join us, Thomas. We're going to follow the yellow brick road. You can be Dorothy and I'll be the scarecrow. Leonard, you can play the green-headed tin man. Bedrock, you're the cowardly lion, and these three dogs can be our three Totos."

"I don't understand," Bedrock said.

"They didn't have televisions in Bedrock's time," Thomas said.

"Are you a communist?" Robin asked Bedrock.

"He was even before the communists, Robin," Thomas said. "We're talking two thousand years ago," Thomas said.

"Oh, I see," Robin said. "Back in the days with Harry Reid and Nancy Pelosi."

Bedrock stared blankly. Leonard threw his hands up in the air and said, "beam me up, Scotty." Then the two men walked away. A stunning woman with long wavy blonde hair and blue-green eyes wearing a white robe and sandals came out of the mist. She was holding hands with a young man in his mid-twenties who was rugged in appearance and dark skinned. She walked up to Bedrock and kissed him. Her voice was soft and her accent was from some place far off.

"My son of many sons, this is my first son, Caleb, and his mother, Chara. She was my first wife." Chara and Caleb hugged Thomas.

"I never met my son until I came to the other side," Bedrock said. Caleb was murdered while he was still connected to his mother inside her belly. He will walk on the earth for the first time when our Master opens the door."

"When?" Thomas asked.

"Only the Father knows," Bedrock answered. "But it is during the time of the third great battle which has already begun. There is much movement from the angels on this side of the in-between and the demons who are trying to steal all the spirits who were created to be with the Father. The demons are jealous of the replacements."

A small group of people appeared from the mist. One was dressed in a captain's uniform from the Civil War era. Another appeared to be a slave from Colonial times. The third man was dressed as an American Indian. And the last man in the group looked like a king from the Celtic period.

"These are some of your ancestors, my son of many sons. They are your fathers. Like me, their spirits were with you every day since you were under the fig tree. Your tree has deep roots and many branches."

A young barefoot woman with jet black eyes and a warm smile joined the group. "Hola, mi hijo," she said. How did you get those blue eyes, mi Tomasito?"

The Irish king stepped forward. "His eyes come from the Irish side of his family."

"And your eyes come from me," Bedrock added. The three dogs interrupted with more requests for petting from Thomas.

"Our son's love for animals comes from our tribe," the Ojibwe Indian said, picking up the chihuahua.

"I hear there's a new son who has chosen a life in the army," the army captain said, extending his arm for a handshake. "I'm Captain James Starkey. When I was your boy's age I was in the army chasing Indians."

The Ojibwe Indian added, "on this side of the

mountain, there's no color or race. We don't chase anyone here. We have no enemies. We're all family. And remember, Starkey of the white ones, you would not be here with your fathers and your grandfathers if you had not smoked the peace pipe with our tribe at the end of your days."

"I can't believe I'm here with my ancestors," Thomas said.

"There are many more waiting for you on the other side of the in-between," Bedrock said. "Are you ready to meet them?"

Suddenly, the ground rumbled from a series of loud tremors.

"What's happening?" Thomas asked. An object appearing bright like a comet whizzed by just above his head followed by thousands more, each wielding shiny long shiny swords.

The Ojibwe clan member turned to Thomas. "That's the great warrior angel, Michael, and his cherubim. We've been waiting for this moment for twenty-four thousand moons. They ride after the four horseman who came to the earth mother to take away the wheat and scorch the land with fireballs on their arrows. The people of the Monsanto tribe fulfilled the prophecy when they altered the seeds making it impossible for the bees to breathe. When the bees died, the famine began. These wars have no winners. That's why our Father is sending back his Son today. It is time to judge the living and the dead."

"Where is Jesus?" Thomas asked.

"He's coming," the Ojibwe answered. "He's in the clouds."

Chapter Sixty-six

The black veil over Marie's face did little to hide the pain she felt. She sat in the front row of the church, flanked by her boys, Patrick and Michael on her right and her daughter, Teresa, on her left. Michael's hands trembled as he looked nervously one last time at the eulogy notes he prepared the night before after the wake was over and the extended family straggled out of the funeral home seemingly unaware how late it was. Michael glanced behind and noticed his godfather, Richard, seated in the row behind him. Richard gave him the classic Morgan seal of approval – a head raise combined with a thumbs up gesture. Michael's mind drifted back to the first time he observed Richard and his dad doing their secret handshake they developed on the playground in elementary school. Michael was rusty but he managed to pull off the handshake when he greeted his godfather the day before.

Two guitars started playing from the upstairs choir as soon as the pall bearers entered from the back of the church. Marie requested the choir be filled with Thomas's relatives, all musicians except for her husband who skipped out on piano lessons so he could spend more time on the tennis courts. Thomas's sister, Sacha, arrived from the airport just in time to take a seat in the choir and practice the opening song an hour before the funeral. She was the youngest of Thomas's siblings and the most free-spirited. She was the one in her immediate family who inherited the singing gene. The crowded church hushed when Sacha and her cousins started singing 'Hallelujah.' All the voices were genetically connected and in perfect harmony. Marie listened to the lyrics and thought about all struggles she had gone through with Thomas. She fidgeted on the cold hard wooden seat as the casket approached. Each Hallelujah sent a shiver down her spine.

Michael cleared his throat when the song ended and he walked up to the podium. He did his best to avoid eye contact with his mother and his siblings so that he could keep his composure. The notes remained in his pocket. "My dad loved that song you just heard. I remember when mom cut his hair with the clippers and she used the wrong setting. Dad had this bald strip on his head. He told mom, 'stop laughing. I promise you someday I'll get back at you. You're gonna pay.' Okay, dad. You win. We played your song and all of us cried when we remembered mom clipping your hair. Now the whole church knows how you are. Or should I say how you were? We know how you sometimes crossed the line and shared too much information about us on Facebook or on your blog. You thought it was pretty funny when you posted pictures of your fake friends, Wilson and Umbro, when the rest of us got tired of your relentless picture taking. For those of you today who don't know about Wilson and Umbro, they're dad's tennis racket and soccer ball he treated like people. My siblings and I cut Wilson's strings and deflated the air out of Umbro this morning before placing them in the casket with our dad. We did this so they can have something to share. You see, they're all broken, just like the song you just heard. Dad lost his legs in a car accident on the way back to Iowa to begin his new life with us. The doctors found cancer while they were treating him for his injuries. I guess that's the part of his life that was described in the song as the minor fall. But there's more to dad's story. It's the major lift. Dad called it faith. He always believed things would work out, even when the economy was bottoming out and Mom told him she was moving out of California with him or without him. Dad saw things other people couldn't see. There's something broken in all of us today. It's the void you left behind, Dad. I'm going to remember what you taught me about faith. And I believe one day you will be raised up from the dead and you will get your legs back. When that happens, Wilson will get his strings back and Umbro will be inflated back to his old self. Then you can play tennis with us and kick soccer balls with us again. I promise you I will keep the faith, Dad. Good-bye. We love you."

Chapter Sixty-seven

"Sir, we're picking up chatter from Iran. Their weapons system just went off-line. They lost all firing capability."

"Who did this? Were they hacked?" The commander asked.

"No, sir. It's similar to what just happened in Israel. Hold on, sir. We have an incoming message from the DMZ in Korea. North Korea ordered a launch of all of its nukes. They were unable to fire. All missile systems are down."

"Mr. President, we need your approval for counter-strikes in Iran and North Korea. We need immediate action before they get their systems back online. Can we launch air strikes against our primary targets?" the commander asked.

All eyes in the situation room turned to the president. He sat there, stone-faced. "There goes my legacy," Hussein said. "Open up my brief case. I'm sending you the codes, commander. We're going nuclear on both targets. Take them out. You have my authorization." Hussein punched his authorization code into the keyboard and slammed the brief case shut while everyone in the room remained silent.

"We're offline," the commander shouted over the speaker phone one minute later. "None of our weapons can fire, Mr. President. We're helpless."

"God bless us," Robinette Smiden said.

"Mr. President, Seal Team 3 is reporting from their position at the Sea of Galilee. You're going to want to hear this, sir. I'm patching them through now. Go ahead, Seal Team 3, give us your report."

"Roger, commander. The center of the cloud above us just tripled in size. Fireballs are spewing out of the cloud and they appear to be flying in organized formations. They are moving outward in every direction. Each fireball has a metal sword attached to it and the front of the fireballs look like faces. The objects appear to be alive, sir."

"What about our man on the ground? Is he approaching you?" the commander asked.

"He was holding his hands up as the objects flew over him. We can hear music coming from the other objects in the sky. There are voices, too. Sir, they're singing Gloria."

Chapter Sixty-eight

This is Fox News with an important update. We are getting reports that UFO's are being spotted above every nation on earth. They have been traced back to a strange funnel cloud over the Sea of Galilee in Israel. Military sources, speaking anonymously off the record because they are not authorized to make a statement have informed us that all military assets from around the world are disabled. This occurred at the same time the cloud appeared above Israel.

"We are live to one of our correspondents on the ground in Tel Aviv. Go ahead, Peter."

"This is Peter Doocy reporting to you live from Tel Aviv, Israel. Everything has shut down here. Cars and buses are stopped in the middle of the streets. People are emptying out from all the buildings around me. Everyone is looking up at the sky."

"Peter, what are the people looking at."

"They appear to be celestial bodies. They are wielding swords in one hand and have trumpets in the other."

"What are these celestial bodies doing?"

"They're all singing in unison. It sounds like they're singing 'Gloria in Excelsis Deo.'"

"What are the people in the streets doing?"

"They're kneeling. Some of them appear to be aiming their camera phones up into the sky. They're video taping the incident."

"Hold on, Peter. We're cutting to Bret Baier in Washington, DC. Go ahead Bret."

"This is Bret Baier standing outside of Congress. It's pandemonium here. Minutes ago we ran outside to see what the loud noises were all about. A line of objects shot across the sky and then spread out about 1,500 feet above us. They appear to be angels that were traveling faster than the speed of sound until they simultaneously came to a screeching halt over our heads. They started singing Gloria in Excelsis Deo. I'm surrounded by members of the House and Senate and other aides."

"Bret, what is everyone doing?"

"They are all kneeling. All vehicles in the area are stopped. People are pouring out onto the streets. Everyone is using their cell phones to photograph the angels while they're kneeling. I've never seen anything like it."

Chapter Sixty-nine

"Commander, what is the status of the countries surrounding Israel? Are your drones seeing the same thing we're seeing in Israel?" the president asked.

"We're not seeing anyone sir."

"What do you mean?" Hussein asked.

"There are no people. Jordan is empty. Syria is empty. Iran is empty with the exception of small groups of people kneeling in the streets. The same is true in Iraq. We don't know where all the people have gone."

"What's the status of our weapons?"

"Mr. President, we have lost control of all weapons."

"Commander, I'm hearing a disturbance outside the situation room. Can you tell me what is going on in Washington?" the president asked.

"Mr. President, you have a multitude of celestial bodies floating above the area. They appear to be singing Gloria."

Robinette Smiden scooted his chair away from the conference table and got down on his knees. Everyone in the room followed except for Hussein. He glared at his vice president and asked, "what the hell are you doing, Robinette?"

"I'm trying to remember the words to the Gloria song," Smiden responded.

Chapter Seventy

"Mom, come quick. You need to see this. There's a seal team in Israel. They're sending live pictures from the Sea of Galilee. It's on every news station. You aren't going to believe this."

Marie rushed in. "Look at all those people, mom. They're walking on water." Michael said.

"There was a man standing there all by himself. He turned around and raised up his hands and then a bright light appeared. It looked like a door opening. Then, all these people started walking out. Look at that man standing there with those three dogs. He looks like dad but he's got legs. And look at the three dogs around him. That's Lady, Lucky and Roxy."

Marie fell to her knees. She kept her eyes focused on the tv screen.

"Look mom, that man in the glowing white robe is speaking," Michael said.

"Turn it louder, Michael, I want to hear him."

Michael turned up the volume and knelt down next to his mother. The man's voice was soft and gentle…

***"Blessed are the poor in spirit,
for theirs is the kingdom of heaven.***

***Blessed are they who mourn,
for they shall be comforted.***

***Blessed are the meek,
for they shall inherit the earth.***

***Blessed are they who hunger and thirst for righteousness,
for they shall be satisfied.***

***Blessed are the merciful,
for they shall obtain mercy.***

***Blessed are the pure of heart,
for they shall see God.***

***Blessed are the peacemakers,
for they shall be called children of God.***

Blessed are they who are persecuted for the sake of righteousness,
for theirs is the kingdom of heaven."

Jesus paused for a moment and then turned back to the bright light. There was one solitary figure lagging behind. Jesus extended his right hand and called out, "Bedrock. Follow me."

~ The Beginning

Made in the USA
Lexington, KY
06 August 2015